SWORD

Sword is first published in English the United Kingdom in 2020 by Corylus Books Ltd, and was originally published in Romanian as Spada in 2008 by Tritonic.

Copyright © Bogdan Teodorescu, 2008
Translation copyright © Sanda Ionescu, 2020

Bogdan Teodorescu has asserted his moral right to be identified as the author of this work in accordance with the Copyright, Designs and Patents Act, 1988.

All rights reserved. No part of this publication may be reproduced in any form or by any means without the written permission of the publisher.
All characters and events portrayed in this publication, other than those clearly in the public domain, are fictitious and any resemblance to real persons, living or not, is purely coincidental.

Corylus Books Ltd

ISBN: 978-1-9163797-2-5

BOGDAN TEODORESCU

SWORD

**Translated from Romanian
by Marina Sofia**

'A noir novel with troubling political implications, as dark and as shocking as they come.'
Le Figaro

CORYLUS
BOOKS

The cast of characters

The President of Romania
The Prime Minister of Romania
The Minister of the Interior
Radu Rădulescu – Leader of the Opposition, former Romanian president
Nenişor Vasile – MP for the Roma Minority
Marinescu – presidential media adviser and speechwriter
Theodor Varlaam – leader of the right-wing National Unity Movement NUM
Presidential special adviser in security matters – seems to have the President's ear
Presidential spokesman – not as good as the President would have wanted
Ion Leşan – the new Minister of the Interior, a stingy Transylvanian
Istrate - Head of Communications and Press Relations at the Presidential Office
Dobre - Under-Secretary at the Romanian Ministry of Foreign Affairs
Vlad – special adviser to the Minister of the Interior
Romuşan - state secretary at the Ministry of Defence
Stoicescu – Head of the Intelligence Services (internal)

Movilă - Commander of the General Directorate of the Bucharest Police, most senior policeman in the capital city

Calin – head of espionage (external intelligence)

Captain Dulgheru – commander of a SWAT team

General Dumbrava – retired from the army, trying to restore it to its former glory

Rotaru – army general and confidante of the Minister of the Interior

Marius Ionescu – belligerent journalist, anti-government

Cârstea – an even more vocal anti-government journalist

Cornel Ardeleanu – a fiery journalist who claims he cannot be bought

Alin Dobrescu – TV host and political interviewer

Adrian Maier – another insubordinate journalist

Mircică – the Presidential Palace's pet journalist

Dan Dumitrescu – a TV reporter

Dr Laurențiu Petre – criminal psychologist and profiler

Sergiu Enescu – political analyst and wily old fox

Andrei Rusu – director of the most powerful private TV channel in Romania

Intrepid Tony – controversial radio show host

Preda – a chat show host

Irina Lascar – a glamorous TV presenter

1

Scorcher of a Sunday summer afternoon, hanging heavily over Obor Market. The heat was keeping people indoors and the market sellers tried to tuck themselves away in the shade of their stalls. You could spot the occasional dodgy sausage grilling on barbeques scattered here and there about the marketplace. A few men lingered over beers at their dirty plastic tables, in no hurry to go home to their wives.

On his habitual corner by the Bucur Obor department store, Nelu the Fly was delivering his usual monotone 'here it is, here it ain't' patter, while moving his matchboxes at lightning speed in front of a small number of blank faces. He'd paid a fortune to be allowed to work in Obor and things weren't going well. That's why he was still trying to make a go of it, though it was the end of market trade and most shoppers had left. Just a few steps away from his table he could spot the little old woman whom he'd tricked out of fifty thousand lei. She'd asked for her money back, but there were too many people around for him to do it openly. He wasn't a bad lad; on the whole he gave money back to those who seemed to be even worse off than him. No point in being harsh with them. But there was something about this old woman that annoyed him. She didn't look like the typical pensioner going for a little flutter. He stole another look in her direction and decided he wouldn't give her a single leu.

He'd learnt all the tricks of the trade from Uncle Fane, but he'd never have that man's dexterity. Plus, Uncle Fane knew how to tell jokes, talk to the customers, get them drunk on words before he even took their money. People would leave him, beaming with satisfaction. While The Fly, he'd nearly been beaten up twice by some heavy-set workmen who lost half a million each in one go – the idiots!

He folded up his table, shooed away the old woman who tried one more time to ask for her money, and set off home. He'd have liked a beer, but the old woman was blocking his access to the bar, weeping and complaining. She clearly had no intention of leaving.

The alleyway behind the department store was shady, so he stopped there for a breather, despite the rank smell. As he was getting ready to leave, he saw a person dressed in a long, greyish-white trench-coat heading towards him. When the figure was no more than a metre or two away, he suddenly swung open the trench-coat, brandished a sword and planted it in The Fly's throat.

2

Less than an hour to go before the close of the evening edition, but the hallways were already quiet. Most people were on holiday, there was barely any real news anyway that month. Victor answered his mobile half-heartedly. Another smartarse who'd learnt how to hide his number when calling.

'Hello, Victor.'

'Hello, Detective, how's life?'

'There's a guy stabbed at the back of Bucur Obor.'

'Who is it?'

'A gypsy. Don't know anything more. But if you send someone asap you'll find them there still.'

'A revenge killing or something?'

'Told you: I don't know yet. Keep in touch.'

An hour later the team got back with a few pictures, predominantly of a puddle of blood, and fragments of a story. The victim, nicknamed The Fly, was approximately 25 years old. He'd been working the Obor area for the past five or six months with his three-card Monte or shell games. He was part of Boy Slit's gang and that was about all they had on him. A local copper told them that he might have owed some money to some guys. He had more than two million lei on him, so he hadn't been robbed. He'd been killed with a knife thrust in the neck. A single blow.

Victor managed to change the front page at the last minute, squeezing in a photo and five brief lines about the crime in Obor. It was by far the most exciting story of the day.

The next day, he spoke to an eyewitness who told him (off the record, of course) that an old woman who'd lost her money playing The Fly's game had cursed him, screaming that he would get it in the neck. He also discovered that The Fly owed a large amount of money to an Armenian gangland boss called Avakian, notorious for trafficking pretty girls. So Victor managed to get another front page out of it, bringing into it the old woman's curse, a larger picture of the crime scene with the pool of blood, the body covered with a black cloth, and with hints that there were some debts, so a moneylender might have had reason to wish The Fly dead.

He sent it all off to print and sought out Avakian, whom he met later that night at the Vox bar opposite the government building. Avakian would not admit whether The Fly owed him any money or not, but suggested they drop this aspect of the story from the papers. His methods for recovering money rather depended on the debtor staying alive. You might scare him a little, send four solid Moldovans to park a coffin in front of his house, or even cut off a finger with a pair of scissors, but why on earth kill him?

At the end of their chat, Avakian paid for the drinks and handed Victor a little envelope full of money. Five thousand dollars to forget the name of the moneylender or indeed the whole hypothesis of a debt killing. On the way home, Victor realised that none of the other papers had mentioned the killing in Obor, which explained the rather large sum of money Avakian had thrown his way. He toyed with the idea of ordering himself an escort, but couldn't be bothered. He was about to fall asleep when his friend the detective called him (got to remember to pay him too!).

'Victor, it's getting serious. We've got another one.'
'Another...?'
'Another gypsy playing his shell games, stabbed in the neck.'
'Where?'
'Southern Market.'
'Another of Slit's boys?'
'Apparently not. Watch out, the TV stations are turning up soon. You'd better hurry if you want to be first.'

The first thing Victor did the following day was to check whether the second victim, nicknamed The Bulgarian, owed any money to Avakian. Unlikely, since he was rich, very rich indeed. He plied his trade because he loved it, not for the money. The Bulgarian drove around in a Mercedes, smuggled alcohol, knew the right people in government, had paid off the police right up to the highest levels, so he had a really comfortable lifestyle. He usually had a band of people running the street games side of things, but every now and then he liked to go out in the marketplace himself to show them how it's done. This last demonstration had cost him dearly.

Victor wrote it up as a separate incident, with a bit of background on The Bulgarian, a well-connected figure in the criminal underworld. To his dismay, the next day, another paper produced the screaming headline 'The Gypsy Killer'.

Bit rich to talk about a serial killer after just two cases!

By the end of the week, however, they had a third. Another gypsy, another guy with criminal connections, small fry, working with girls brought over from Moldova and the Ukraine. He'd been found on the ring road on the outskirts of Bucharest with his throat cut. Probably caught out while he was collecting his dues from the girls carrying out their business.

3

Istrate, Head of Communications and Press Relations at the Presidential Office, was having what he liked to call 'a fucked-up sort of day'. He'd only just got back from his summer holidays on a boring old Greek island and there was far too much work piled up in his office. He was trying to catch up with the press summaries for the past ten days, but he couldn't quite work up his appetite for them. The only things he liked about his job were the drinks receptions and parties held at the Presidential Palace, as well as the trips abroad. Watching the sickly sweet smiles of Romanian officials sucking up to the President, the meaningless small talk over dinner, hasty shopping trips with the limo waiting outside, being greeted by the guard of honour whenever you landed in a new country – all of this made up for the exhausting and dull work that made up the greater part of his job.

He couldn't stand the Romanian journalists. They just didn't seem to respect him enough, always seemed to prod him with tricky questions and launch personal attacks against him. He didn't like to admit it, but he knew only too well that he'd only got the job thanks to his mother, who was a close friend of the President.

He was about to give up on even pretending to work and have a wander through the shops instead – he was rather fond of buying suits – when a young press officer brought in a new summary of today's newspapers. The main news story seemed to be a serial killer targeting gypsies. He skimread it and decided that the July heat had got to his colleagues. Whatever next? A press summary about rapists and paedophiles?

He was briefly tempted to write a report complaining about the lack of professionalism in his team. Instead of getting reports about major problems, the international situation, global crises that could destabilise the Balkan region, an in-depth political analysis, he had to put up with silly homicide stories! He gave up reading the press summary, but resolved to complain about it the next time he met the President. Speaking of which, it had been more than five months since they'd last met.

The truth was, the President couldn't stand him. He'd even set up another press office, running in parallel, so that he wouldn't have too much to do with Istrate. This second press office had already informed the President of the three murders, as well as the official statement produced in response by the Union of Romas.

The President liked to position himself internationally as a protector of ethnic minorities in his country, so he was very sensitive about this topic. He felt this issue could cause huge problems.

SWORD

The Minister of the Interior had given his personal assurance that the culprit would be caught before the end of the week. He had forgotten to mention, however, if they actually had a suspect or if they'd at least identified a reason for the killings. There were only two things that the three victims had in common: they were all gypsies, and they'd all been in trouble with the law.

The President was about to jet off for a five-day visit in the Caucasian region, to discuss yet again the possibility of an oil pipeline that he'd have liked to see pass through Romania, rather than Turkey or Bulgaria. He was sure the case would be resolved by the time he got back.

Just as he was sitting down on board his Airbus 313, the President was informed that a fourth body had been found. Another gypsy, another criminal, with his throat cut, but no other connection to the previous three victims.

4

Four throats cut in just a few days. It was enough to make Iliescu, the VP of the Romanian Foundation for the Protection of Human Rights, return early to Bucharest from annual leave, leaving his wife and daughters to fend for themselves in the seaside resort of Neptun.

With the president of the foundation on a training course in the States, and as VP, he could no longer ignore the various Roma leaders who'd contacted international organisations for the protection of ethnic minorities. They were all now, in turn, demanding explanations from him.

For Iliescu it was perfectly clear that it was a vendetta between the police and the Roma population, and that the Romanian state had decided to turn a blind eye. He was a closet homosexual and had experienced for himself the state's tendency to discriminate against minorities of all kinds. But this time there would be an international outcry. After all that had happened in Bosnia and Kosovo, no one in Europe would tolerate such excesses against any minority.

He sent off various faxes to his contacts abroad, then he wrote an appeal in six languages on the home page of the Foundation's website: **Stop the Genocide of Minorities in Romania**. This strategy had been successful previously, although in that case it had referred exclusively to the gay community. He'd managed to provoke a bit of a scandal all around Europe, the highlight being a demonstration by LGBTQ organisations in the UK calling for a ban of the sale of Romanian wines in British supermarkets. Although he couldn't openly admit the part he'd played in that success story, he was nevertheless extremely proud of it.

He was annoyed that in this instance the papers were keen to report the cruder, more sensationalist side of things, rather than focus on the human rights being trampled. Not a single representative of any organisation for the protection of human rights had been interviewed. All you had were puff pieces from politicians and the police, who were obviously colluding with the killer. Worst of all, there was even one tabloid with a headline screaming – in red – **The Sword of Justice for Us All!**

He started writing an open letter to that tabloid, pointing out that the international courts of justice condemn not only those who commit physical acts of violence towards minorities, but also their moral accomplices, meaning those who incite hatred through speech or publication.

'The only thing this ethnic group is guilty of is that they are a minority in a country where the majority are against their very existence. This majority is determined to get rid of them to the sound of overwhelming applause. Other minorities would do well to not stand by passively and to remember that it might be them next.'

He sent off the complaint to the tabloid, then, for good measure, to all the other papers and TV stations.

Then he got into an argument with the PA of the Foundation's president, who thought the text was too incendiary, and would therefore have preferred to consult with her boss before sending it off. But it was three in the morning in the US and her boss had switched off his mobile.

5

There were precisely two reasons why the Minister of the Interior was furious. Firstly (and most importantly), he'd been recalled from his holidays by the President, who'd phoned him from the plane taking him to Azerbaijan. Secondly, all the newspapers seemed to have more information than he did about the case.

For example, it was from the papers that he found out that the throat-cutting hadn't been done with an ordinary knife, but with a sword or dagger. The head of the Forensic Institute confirmed this was true, and that his institute had put together a report about this from the second murder onwards. The report, which stated that the blade was thicker and longer than a standard knife, was leaked to the papers before reaching the Minister's desk. It also contained an analysis of the precise thrust – the killer was obviously well trained in using the weapon. The Ministry of the Interior kept a close eye on all the fencing clubs and martial arts training centres in the area. The speculation that this could be a ninja sword was instantly discarded by the Forensic Institute: this was a weapon with a much broader blade than a ninja one.

Another thing the Minister found out from the papers was that a little old lady had quarrelled with the first victim, because he'd refused to give back her money, and that she'd cursed him to die before the end of the day.

The most explosive thing the Minister read that day was the letter written by a woman as a sort of reply to the open letter published by the VP of the Romanian Foundation for Protection of Human Rights. The woman, who asked to remain anonymous, said that two years ago she had been kidnapped, raped and forced to become a prostitute by the third victim. She'd been locked up in a house somewhere in a slum of Bucharest, watched over by the victim's mother and sisters, and forced to have sexual intercourse with over thirty men. So, as far she was concerned, the killer was a saviour, not a criminal.

The Secret Services files that the Minister glanced through that morning revealed that all four victims had criminal records and each had been in prison at least once in their lives. So that might make one think that the killer either knew somebody in the police force, or was an ex-copper or – heaven forbid! – still was a policeman. The files indicated that this was not only a serial killer, but clearly a vigilante. Given the deterioration of the relationship between the Romanian majority and a small proportion of the Roma community, this type of vigilante justice might be welcomed by a large section of the general population. Furthermore, the files warned that well-armed mafia gangs might be ready and willing to take revenge. The appendix contained a list of the most violent gypsy mafia families.

The Minister of the Interior did not have a lot of people he could trust in the senior police ranks. He considered them generally corrupt and inefficient. So he asked for the help of an army general and the head of the Intelligence Services. He met them at his official residence in Snagov. He also invited the Commander of the General Directorate of the Bucharest Police to the meeting, the only policeman he could bear.

'Sir, you have to be mindful this is dangerous territory. Public opinion...' ventured intelligence head Stoicescu.

'Yes, I get it, I read the Secret Service files. But I've got far more than public opinion to worry about. This is a pre-election year. The EU will be checking up on us in autumn again. In four months' time, we'll be hosting the OSCE Summit. I've got two main concerns. One, that this chap with his sword continues with his killing spree. Secondly, that we won't catch him in time. So we could end up with mass demonstrations organised by the gypsies in front of the Parliament building just as the OSCE is convening. And we could end up with revenge attacks and retaliations by both the gypsies and the Romanians. All we need is another riot like we had in 1993 in Hădăreni or in 1991 in Bolintin, but this time in the capital!'

'What strikes me as bizarre is the lack of a coherent message...' General Rotaru was the senior participant, with a long track record of military diplomacy. 'The killer, The Sword, as the press has been quick to label him, clearly intends to send a message. His victims are all criminals and gypsies. But they all worked in different areas, they never collaborated or had things in common... It appears he chooses his victims somewhat haphazardly. That's why I don't think he's an experienced criminal. I bet he doesn't have a criminal record anywhere with the police.'

Commander Movilă of the Bucharest Police was keeping very quiet that evening. It was clear that everyone else was blaming him and his officers for not having any leads regarding the identity of the killer. He could feel it in his gut, that there would be further dead bodies, precisely because the killer chose his victims at random, and because Bucharest was full of gypsies with criminal links. He could hear the warning issued by the Minister loud and clear: quick results were desired. And if the results failed to materialise, then his head would be one of the first on the chopping block.

'I wouldn't worry so much about the reactions in the West,' General Rotaru continued, 'The crimes of a psychopath don't concern them. They are more interested in how the government reacts to this.'

'And if the government can't catch the psychopath?'

'A few heads rolling at all levels in the police force should demonstrate the government is taking things seriously. Admittedly, it also demonstrates how incompetent the police are, but no one worries about that too much. After all, the Belgians were unable to find their pedophile for years and years.'

Stoicescu interjected that the open letter by Iliescu accused the government of being complicit in this whole situation.

'That mad dog poofter, let him bark!' the general said drily, 'Of course, it's been quiet, because most people are still away on holiday. But if you don't manage to catch him by the end of the holiday season, then there will be fireworks in Parliament and in the press from September onwards. I wouldn't worry about the audience abroad, however.'

'If you could only convince the President of that…'

'I've tried to explain that to him many times. But his special advisers have a different agenda. A well-oiled agenda, I might add…' And the general made that well-known gesture of rubbing two fingers and a thumb together, which for hundreds of years had been a synonym for corruption in Romania.

Stoicescu was about to add something about the presidential advisers who had rather close, possibly illegal relationships with foreign security services, but the Minister broke in.

'I had no idea that Iliescu is gay. Doesn't he have kids? His younger daughter is in the same class as my son…'

'Maybe Mrs Iliescu is on very good terms with her neighbours then,' General Rotaru replied cheerfully.

6

Marin Poloboc, nicknamed Cudgel thanks to the impressive size of his hands, was not shy about using his fists. During Ceaușescu's era, he'd been incarcerated twice for being a little too enthusiastic about beating up debtors. Under capitalism, however, he'd become quite the entrepreneur, working as a bailiff and a bodyguard.

He was currently looking after a girl of fourteen, the daughter of a rich Roma he'd met in prison. Back in those days, the Roma lad was nothing to write home about, but since then he'd struck it rich with cigarette smuggling. Cudgel himself was Moldovan, but he'd been living in Bucharest for so many years now that he'd completely lost his accent. He wasn't terribly fond of Romas in general, but his boss seemed a quiet, decent sort. He did get nasty when drunk and rumour had it that he couldn't quite get it up anymore, so he would punish his women for that. But he paid them well afterwards, so everyone seemed reasonably content.

Cudgel's only mission was to look after the daughter. He took her to school, to ballet classes, to the swimming pool, shopping. Two weeks ago, his boss took him to one side just as he was about to go home and said that he'd got into trouble with some Arabs and was scared that they might try to kidnap his daughter. He was going to send her abroad, in secret. Such a great secret that not even Cudgel was allowed to know where.

While the girl was away, Cudgel was supposed to be looking after the man himself. Less than a week ago, his boss had asked him if he had three or four friends who were handy with weapons. He found about five, his boss hired three of them and gave them handguns.

Two days ago, his boss finally let his guard down a little and went to see one of his regular squeezes, the beautiful blonde Diana. He entered her block of flats at eleven at night and didn't come out again. The lads waited for him all night in the car outside, then finally went up to knock at the door at ten the next morning. All they found in the flat was their dead boss. No blonde to be seen. That's when they discovered that the block of flats had a back exit.

Although the MO was very different in this case, the papers considered this to be the fifth victim of the serial killer. What other conclusion could be drawn, when the dead guy was a gypsy with a criminal record? The police preferred to spend their time searching for the blonde lady in whose flat the crime had taken place. By a stroke of luck, the papers hadn't found out about her. Meanwhile, Cudgel and the other guys mentioned an Arab connection – and there definitely hadn't been anything linking the first four victims to the Arabs.

No, clearly this latest incident was probably more about settling an account via a contract killer, rather than a vigilante calling himself The Sword. After all, who'd have put out a contract on someone like The Fly?

Besides, the murder weapon was a plastic bag, not a sword. The victim had died of suffocation, not a cut throat.

7

A guy wanders around Bucharest with a medieval weapon and knocks off people. Five and counting. What possible motive could he have? Maybe it's some kind of revenge. Maybe someone in his family suffered at the hands of gypsies. Or maybe he himself did. Maybe he's just after the publicity... Which he's certain to get from these asinine tabloids, who make me ashamed of my profession as a journalist, and that my paper lies next to them on the same newsstand. Or maybe he's a madman. Someone who thinks he's on a divine mission, that someone is whispering in his ear that he should kill.

*Actually, I don't care about his motives at all. All I care about is the fact that, although we have five victims, the Romanian state seems incapable of doing anything. The President is off gallivanting in some godforsaken countries to try and capture that title that no one cares about: 'leader of the Balkans'. He practises his personal banter with the planet's great political leaders in his bathroom mirror. Then he rushes to phone the Minister of the Interior from the steps to his plane, which finally gets **that** lazy bastard to shift his bulk from his nice little deckchair in the sun on some Mediterranean island. So* *the Minister gets back home to a country that gives him far too easy a ride, politically speaking.*

I bet that Romanian politicians have watched far too many rubbish American films and think the country can be governed while you are rushing about on your private jet from one end of the world to another. They're convinced that all the problems in this country can be resolved by those self-important statements that you give when you land or take off at Otopeni Airport.

Other countries have criminals as well. What do you expect, that we will be spared any murderers in our country because our President is an important regional leader? The difference is that in other countries, the criminals get caught and punished. And even in those rubbish films, when it becomes clear that politicians are incapable of doing their job, they at least have the common sense to resign. Clearly, our Romanian politicians are so worn out by their world tours that they fall asleep during the crucial part of those films.

The President lowered the press report and glared at the two advisers who were still there with him at this late hour.

'I've been telling you guys for two years to watch out for this Marius Ionescu guy. Two years. And this rag that he writes for. If you can't handle him, then at least get rid of this paper of his.'

The special adviser on security matters was taking notes. He seemed to write down every single word that dropped from his leader's lips. The other adviser, the presidential spokesman, knew that he was in hot water. He'd been a journalist before joining the presidential palace, which his boss seemed to think should give him a free rein with all the media.

'Have you spoken to this Ionescu?' the President asked him.

'Many times, Mr. President. He says his paper won't sell if he praises you.'

'I don't want his praise. I just want to be left alone! What have those crimes got to do with me? Do they expect me to catch the culprit personally? Protect Bucharest's gypsies myself? I haven't had a day off in three years. I went to Azerbaijan to try and salvage the pipeline project. Things are going badly and we have to consider emergency measures. I can't handle everything myself. If I could handle the press myself, I'm sure we wouldn't have any problems. But I can't – and you are clearly incapable of doing your job properly! If you'd done your job as it's supposed to be done, then there should have been a chorus of condemnation from all the other papers over Marius Ionescu's article. There should have been readers' letters flooding in from all over the country: from intellectuals, from student unions, from everyone. Readers cancelling their subscriptions. Advertising agencies refusing to pay for ads as long as Marius Ionescu still writes for that paper. Oh, by the way, we have to send a press release about how important our trip to Azerbaijan was…'

'We've already done that, Mr. President.'

'Well, where is it then? No one's published it! I want to see it splashed all over the front pages! And I want you to call a press conference right now.'

'Regarding…?'

'This murderer, of course.'

'Mr. President,' the security adviser intervened timidly, 'I don't think that's a good idea. I've spoken to the secret services and the police – they don't have anything concrete… On the contrary, there are rumours that the police might be behind it all.'

'And what? You expect me to allow people to attack me because the police can't do their jobs properly?'

'It's only Marius Ionescu who's attacking you. The other papers are neutral, or even sympathetic towards you.'

'For the time being. This state of affairs has to be nipped in the bud! I want you to release a statement that the fifth murder has nothing to do with the first four. That will discredit Ionescu, show the world he's a crap journalist. We have to destroy the credibility of those who try to act against us. And find something which will compromise him. Please talk to Stoicescu and Calin, see if they can dig up some dirt on him. If it's war this Marius Ionescu guy wants, I'll give him war! And tell Mircică to write a thorough analysis of the Azerbaijan trip.'

'He wrote about it earlier today…'

'Tell him to write it again! To counteract Ionescu's poison.'

'Yes, sir, but Ionescu's paper has the largest circulation in the country, while Mircică's is tiny. It won't help at all. Plus, everyone seems to know that Mircică is our pet journalist, who will write whatever we tell him to write.'

SWORD

The President refused to engage any further. After a short pause, he simply repeated that he wanted a press release about the fifth crime, and then left the room to get some rest, followed by his security adviser. The latter had been remarkably silent during the previous discussion, but now he let rip.

Mr President must have noticed how inefficient his spokesman was, that he seemed to lack even the most basic journalistic contacts, and didn't care at all about the quality of his work. Add to that his ever-increasing alcohol consumption and his adulterous relationship with a TV news presenter…

And let's not forget the head of the Intelligence Service Stoicescu, who never seems to come up with any of the goods demanded by the President's office. He must have some documents against Ionescu somewhere, he thought. Hadn't he built a mountain chalet with money received from an Arab trader in counterfeit goods? Doesn't he have an offshore account in Cyprus and a flourishing business importing medical equipment? His wife and daughters are constantly jetting off on expensive holidays abroad. There must be something illegal in all that, but the Head of Intelligence refuses to help us. Meanwhile, Calin, the head of the espionage agency, would love to help them, but he doesn't have any information on Ionescu. As for the serial killer situation – the main problem there was the Minister of the Interior…

'You know he hates you, sir, he's never been one of your supporters. Plus, he's totally out of it. My contacts in the ministry tell me he's doing sod-all about finding the assassin. If he can't find the killer in two weeks, he should be forced to resign. That would show them how committed you are to the case. That would show them your genuine leadership qualities.'

'I agree. If there's no progress within the next couple of days, then some heads will have to roll. I suppose I'll have to speak to Stoicescu personally. I hate people who forget who placed them in certain functions. Does he think that he'll keep his job if I lose the next elections? Is that why he's sucking up to the opposition? OK, if we don't organise a press conference, maybe we can at least call some of the press barons to the office and give them an informal briefing? Excluding Marius Ionescu, of course, or anyone from his rag.'

By that point, the spokesman had returned with the press statement. The President made one or two minor edits, checked if they'd spoken to their pet journalist and if there was a risk of any further attacks.

'Actually, I just wanted to tell you that there's been some flooding in the north of the country. It might be a good idea to send some aid in the region and report about it in the press. Perhaps even go and pay them a visit…'

8

I personally never understood why politicians suddenly start fearing the press once they get the top jobs. When they're in opposition or when don't have a ministerial portfolio, they are a model of cooperation, courting journalists, calling them, always having time to answer their questions. And they always say that they won't repeat the mistakes of their predecessors when they get into power. Then they get into power and – would you believe it? Suddenly they're unavailable, the press is public enemy no. 1, any journalists who are even faintly critical of them should be fired… Every personal attack becomes a danger to national security, and they want to re-examine the freedom of the press.

Three years ago, at an international roundtable organised by the BBC, I noticed that Romanian political leaders had a bit of a nostalgia for party presses. Newspapers that would praise them. So they try to create papers which will sing their praises once they come to power. I don't want to attack anyone purely for the sake of attacking them, but surely it's the duty of the press to ring alarm bells if necessary. Politicians don't need paeans of praise for doing their jobs; they need to be held accountable.

When it comes to the recent serial killer news story, my paper has not been as sensationalist as many of the others. The President, however, decided to teach us to suck eggs. We received an unbelievably patronising press release, stating that the serial killer has killed 'only' four, not five people so far. Let's examine this in a bit more detail. This press release was obviously created by someone from the presidential stable of special advisers and was sent in response to the article written by Marius Ionescu three days ago. I've always appreciated Ionescu's robust style, although I don't personally agree with the political slant of his publication. In this instance, I would go so far as to say that I believe Marius Ionescu was mistaken. The President of the Republic has nothing to do with a common criminal. You expect the police to catch him and the justice system to punish him. It would be infantile to expect the President to play private detective in the darkest corners of the capital's parks.

Unfortunately, by intervening personally and stating that there were four not five crimes, the President has given ample grist to the mill for Ionescu. If the President personally clarifies the number of murders, then why the hell do we need a ministry of the interior, a police force or a prosecution service? If the President stands up and plays detective, then what's the point of paying for investigators and criminal experts? The President has proved once more – for the how many-eth time in his (hopefully brief) political career – that he can deliver an official communiqué that is of zero interest to anyone.

Not to mention the triumphalist reporting about the trip to Azerbaijan, which came out at the same time as the aforementioned press release.

Yes, Marius Ionescu was wrong to demand that the President take personal responsibility for the case of the serial killer, but he pays for his own mistakes, in the pages of his own paper. The President makes mistakes that we the taxpayers have to pay for, gets his personal fan club to publish things at our expense and then has the nerve to try to teach me lessons about unbiased reporting!

So I hereby announce that I will boycott any personal invitation to Cotroceni. I have nothing to say to a man who thinks he knows more about journalism than any of the professionals.

'How on earth did this godawful Cârstea know about the planned gathering at Cotroceni? This place leaks like a sieve, I can't stand it! Not only do I have to watch my back and whisper, because the close personal protection guys hate my guts. Now I can't even trust my closest collaborators. There were just three of us in the room when we discussed inviting the journalists to an informal briefing! Three! And Cârstea splashes it all over his paper, attacks me and destroys every bit of credibility I have. The other journalists will now refuse to come to the briefing, because they'll think I invited Cârstea before I invited them. How dare he turn me down! How on earth do I recover from this one? Your job, as my special advisers, is to get me out of shit, not pile it on me! Last time I looked, it was only Ionescu attacking me – now we've got Cârstea too! Whoever next?'

'But Mr. President, sir...' the spokesman tried to get a word in edgeways.

'When I gave you the job, you told me you were on excellent terms with Cârstea. That he'd been your professor at journalism school, that you were his favourite student...'

'Well, he feels that you've become very distant since becoming president...'

'Yes, I've become distant from my wife too. But she doesn't go around writing nasty opinion pieces, does she? Of course I've grown distant. When you're in opposition, you've got time for journalists. When you're in power, you're too busy with other things. Do you know what demands your dear friend Cârstea made as soon as I became president? He wanted no less than five ambassadorial positions for his friends, including the UK. I managed to get him two and he got all huffy. Now he's attacking me. Let's recall those two ambassadors – Tunisia and the Philippines, I believe they were. That way, he's at least got a proper reason to get mad at me.'

The security adviser wrote a quick note in his diary to try to prevent this at all costs. The Foreign Minister had been very upset with the way the President had overruled his own nominations for those two posts. He'd be livid to see yet another sudden change of heart. As for the presidential spokesman, well, his career was clearly down the drain. The President might not fire him immediately, but he would almost certainly be given a dead-end job, such as director of the National Audiovisual Council or a minor diplomatic post. The Minister of the Interior would follow suit shortly. Gradually, he would be able to start getting rid of the driftwood surrounding the President.

9

Ol' Staté used to be the most elegant of ticket hawkers, always dressed in a suit, with a clean white shirt and a matching tie. In winter he would wear a long black coat, with a white silk scarf. He was always polite to clients, even when he was ripping them off over ticket prices, which fluctuated wildly, depending on how popular certain shows were.

When a new film came out, Ol' Staté would watch it that very first morning, so he could talk knowledgeably about it to clients. People paid good money, they deserved to be well informed about what they were watching. He'd never had any trouble with the police, even during the Ceaușescu years. He'd developed a whole network of ticket reselling, including arthouse cinemas and theatre shows. All the people who worked for him were polite and well-dressed. If any of them so much as raised their voice, they'd be kicked out on the spot.

In 1989 he married a girl of sixteen. He was forty at the time and there was pressure on him to start a family. The wedding had been the highlight of the neighbourhood. Then the revolution came and things started going wrong. After three years the ticket hawking business had all but died out: nobody was going to the cinema or the theatre anymore. They were just propped up in front of the TV or off demonstrating somewhere.

He tried setting up his own business, but to no avail. He ended up selling music CDs and DVDs in front of the Unirea department store. He occasionally used his rhetorical skills to persuade reluctant buyers, but things had changed. His shirts were no longer clean, he often left his suit at home ... and home itself had become a bit of nightmare. His wife was now twenty-six and he was over fifty. When the money disappeared, she started causing trouble.

Now that he was out and about most of the day, rumour had it that she'd started an affair with some wise guy from the neighbourhood. He nearly caught them at it one evening, and his wife didn't even bother to deny it. The neighbours were clearly talking behind his back. One of them, who'd just moved into the neighbourhood, had dared to ask him how his daughter was. How could he admit that it wasn't his daughter, it was his wife? To avoid seeing her and getting all upset, he would go and watch a film in the evening, after returning his remaining stash to the warehouse. He'd get home after ten. She would yell at him that she had no money, that she wanted to go on holiday, then turn her back on him and fall asleep.

He'd watched his father die in an alcoholic coma, so he never touched a drop himself. His drug of choice was a good film. But that evening, he didn't fancy going to the cinema. It had been such a hot day, all he wanted was a shower and a cold glass of water. He left the CDs and DVDs at the warehouse, signed the papers and set off home. He fell asleep on the metro and woke up two stops further down the line.

When he finally got home, red and blue lights were flashing outside his block of flats. There were four police cars, an ambulance and a whole bunch of rubberneckers. As he got closer, he heard one of his neighbours living on the ground floor tell the police that there he was, Angelica's husband. He felt faint.

The policeman grabbed him. Where was he coming from, where had he been for the past three hours, could anyone vouch for him? Staté tried to find out what was going on, but the policeman just kept droning on and on that he'd better confess. A plainclothes detective also showed up and asked the same questions. He replied he'd been at work, explained about the CDs and signing off.

He gave them his number, and luckily one of the neighbours confirmed his alibi. What had happened with Angelica? Nothing to her personally, but the guy she'd been in bed with had been stabbed in the neck. A neighbour found him propped up against the communal bins between the second and third stairwell. Dead.

She was forty-five but looked at least sixty. Summer or winter, she always wore all of her clothes on top of each other, including a sort of pink woollen turban to hide her greasy hair. She would go up to people with her begging hand, muttering some kind of prayer the words of which she'd long forgotten. In spite of her disgusting appearance, and the fact that she spent half the day in a drunken stupor, she managed to make enough money. Maybe people just gave her something to get rid of her. The street vendors called her Keyhole, but her actual name was Maria. She'd worked for fifteen years at the textile factory, mostly the night shift. It was so darn cold that she started drinking and so, bit by bit, she ended up on park benches or drunk in the ditch. Her husband had become so ashamed of her that he kicked her out.

The textile factory had closed down, not that they'd have wanted her back. She tried begging in front of churches or at the railway station, but got beaten up by those who felt she was intruding on their patch. Then she got to know Costi and was now under his protection. She had to give him all the money she earned, and in return he looked after her, fed her and even gave her some pocket money for drinks. She had tried to keep more of the money for herself once, but that didn't work out. Some beggar kids told Costi and he gave her such a savage kicking that she never attempted it again. It was fine with just the pocket money. Better than being beaten up. And during the summer, she could start her job early.

Costi usually appeared around noon, leaning against a phone box, smoking. If he was pleased with the amount she gave him, he'd offer her a cigarette. If not, he'd take the money without a word and go to collect from others. He'd pass by again late afternoon, just before she left. There was no point begging in the evening – no one gave anything then.

But today she hadn't seen him at all. Not at noon, not in the evening. Quite lucky really, since she hadn't made much money and he'd have been annoyed. The next day one of his mates showed up instead of him and told her that he'd be the one collecting money from now on, because Costi had been killed.

10

The Chamber of Deputies in the Romanian parliament was usually not very well attended on a Monday afternoon, but this time it was packed with MPs and journalists. The MP for the Roma Minority, Nenişor Vasile, was itching to ask the Minister of the Interior some tough questions and they all had an inkling what those questions were going to be about.

Although he only had the one vote, Nenişor punched well above his weight, not least because of his very close relationship with the leader of the main opposition party. Everyone suspected that if that party were to win the next elections, Nenişor would occupy a prime spot in the Cabinet. Besides, nobody could ignore the more than two million votes of the ethnic Romas. Of course, no one could control those votes either, but Nenişor seemed far more likely to reunite them than any of the other politicians.

'Mr. Speaker, my fellow parliamentarians. I am here today to address the Minister of the Interior, but also to make a political statement. Over the past twenty-five days, six (some say seven) Romas have been viciously killed. They left behind them eleven orphans and were often the sole breadwinner in their families. The way in which they have been assassinated shows premeditation – and they've been targeted purely because of their ethnicity…'

'And criminal activities…' someone shouted from the government coalition side of the room.

'It's far more of a criminal activity to privatise vast sectors of the economy to your preferred people, simply so you can pocket the bribes!' Nenişor used his microphone for maximum impact, and the MPs of the opposition parties burst into applause.

The Speaker asked for silence, to allow the Roma MP to continue.

'I know you don't love us! We are nothing but dirty gypsies for you. I see that in the looks you give me every single day. No matter that I am well educated, have a Ph.D. in science, am married with three children, have done my military service and have paid taxes all my life. I'm still nothing but a gypsy to you. I've been suffering these humiliations since childhood, humiliations that you can never truly understand. My father, God rest his soul, also had to endure this persecution, although he too had gone to university and was well-known internationally for his scientific research. Since becoming an MP, I've been advising the Roma community to integrate, to move beyond their exceptional status. Thus far, you have to admit that we've actually been a relatively quiet ethnic minority. We don't demand bilingual signposting, our own schools and universities, lots of special rights. We don't complain to all the different

European commissions. But this has gone too far! Six Romas have been killed, for no other reason – I repeat, for NO other reason – than the fact that they are Roma, and nobody can be bothered to find the culprit. According to my sources, the Minister of the Interior has given instructions that this case is not a high priority. I wonder why? Had it been six ethnic Hungarians or six Romanians, this would have been top priority, wouldn't it? But no need to rush things for mere gypsies! Well, I would advise you to hurry up … if you don't want to see an angry gypsy. Or one who is frightened to death.'

By this point, the government coalition MPs had drowned out the voice of the Roma representative. The opposition MPs shouted back, the speaker tried to calm everyone down, while Nenișor was yelling at the Minister of the Interior, demanding that he share the results of the investigation to date.

Of course, he wasn't expecting the Minister to talk about an ongoing investigation, but he'd dropped a ticking bomb in their midst. The risk of an interethnic conflict (which hadn't really crossed the minds of anyone up to that moment) suddenly concentrated the minds of those in power. After all, who could afford anything like that in the Balkans, after Kosovo, and just as they were portraying themselves abroad as a stable country in the region?

11

The TV presenter whose glacial professional smile graced the TV screens every evening was rehearsing the questions she planned to ask him live. Then she returned to her teleprompter.

The production assistant checked his mike again and hid the wire under his jacket. A lively young lady patted down his face with a powder puff. It was very hot in the studio and it was Petre's first TV appearance. The studio fell silent, the news intro music came on and the presenter started speaking.

'Good evening. As reported earlier, this weekend two further bodies were discovered in Bucharest, believed to be the latest in the series of killings committed by the assassin the press have nicknamed Sword. Our local reporter Dan Dumitrescu is here with the latest details from the Forensic Institute. Good evening, Dan.'

'Good evening, Irina. Good evening, ladies and gentlemen. According to official sources at the Forensic Institute, it is almost certain that the latest two victims, Vasile Plesa, known as Sile the Butcher in the criminal underworld, and Costi Dumitru, were killed by the same perpetrator who has killed at least four other people in the past twenty-five days. Both Plesa and Dumitru were of Roma origin, as were the other four victims, and both had a criminal record. Both of them were killed through a single blow with a sharp object. Our forensic experts believe the killer to be skilled at handling this type of weapon, given the precision of the incision. Over to you, Irina.'

'Are there any developments regarding the possible identity of the killer?'

'For the time being, the Bucharest Police and the Ministry of the Interior have been obstinately silent. Our sources tell us that there are four investigative teams handling the case.'

'Are the victims' families there, at the Forensic Institute? What can you tell us about the situation there?'

'Twenty-five minutes ago Roma minority MP Nenișor Vasile arrived at the Institute. He accused the press of collusion with the killer and then rejoined the families of the victims for a private conversation. As far as we understand, the two of them will have a joint funeral, and several thousand Romas from Bucharest and surroundings are expected to attend the ceremony.'

'Thank you, Dan. Meanwhile, back in the studio, we've invited forensic psychologist Laurențiu Petre in our studio, to give us an insight into the mind of the killer. Good evening, Dr Petre.'

'Good evening.'

'What is the meaning of these killings? What drives the killer, do you think?'

'I would like to start with a couple of caveats. First of all, we don't know yet if it's a single killer, a couple or even a group. Recent history…'

'Are you saying it could be more than one killer?'

'Well, yes. Serial killings are often the work of more than one perpetrator. But what is of interest here is not the number of killers – which our colleagues at the forensic institute will no doubt be able to determine soon – but what motivates the killer or killers. Research shows that there are three types of serial killers: the visionaries, the vigilante and the hedonist.'

'Could you explain?'

'Of course. The visionaries kill because there's a voice in their head that urges them to do so, and they often suffer from severe behavioural or hallucinatory problems. Vigilantes kill because they want to purge society of evil, or because they want to get revenge for a trauma experienced by them or a loved one. The hedonist kills simply for pleasure. There are some other sub-categories of course, such as the serial husbands who kill their wives so they can inherit their wealth. But in this case, I believe we have the vigilante type killer or group of killers. There are a couple of links between the victims which makes us believe this to be the case. First of all, they are all ethnic Roma. Secondly, all of them have a criminal record and – if I remember correctly – have served prison sentences. So we have a certain algorithm for selecting the victims: Roma with criminal records. Why are they doing it? Several possible reasons. Maybe he was humiliated by Romas in his childhood. Or maybe someone in his family fell victim to a Roma criminal. Or he could possibly be Roma himself...'

'The assassin could be Roma?'

'Yes. In that case, he's more likely to be a visionary. For example, there was the case of an Amerindian – Native American, as they call them nowadays – who killed prostitutes of Native American origin because he wanted to keep their race pure. Our killer could be a Roma purging his ethnic group of its criminal elements.'

'You've heard how the Roma MP accused the government and the police of inaction. What do you think he is going to think of your statement, that it could very well be a Roma killer?'

'I don't know what he'll think. But I do want to tell you that serial killers are often very intelligent, manipulative, and able to protect themselves. It is hard to catch them anywhere in the world. One of the most famous serial killers in the world, Ted Bundy, was only caught after five years. During that time, he went on to kill over a hundred women. You see, the trouble is that serial killers appear to be perfectly ordinary, your typical boy next door. So I think we should leave politics out of this criminal investigation.'

'Thank you, Dr Petre, for joining us here tonight. We will return with other news after a short commercial break.'

When the adverts started, Irina shook his hand and promised he'd be invited again. A skimpily-dressed young lady accompanied him downstairs. As he was about to leave the TV station, he saw Irina reappear onscreen to announce that the police had discovered another body fitting the pattern of the previous six victims in a garage in Balta Albă.

12

The Minister of the Interior was sitting in his darkened dining room, a glass of Scotch in his hand, apparently riveted by the Discovery Channel. It was a programme about William of Normandy landing in Pevensey Bay in 1066. King Harold II was waiting for him just outside Hastings, but his army was exhausted after a prior confrontation with the Vikings. And then William tricked the last Saxon king by getting his infantry to simulate panic…

The phone rang just as he was following the final attack of the Norman cavalry.

'Are you watching Preda's show?' his communications adviser asked him without any introduction.

'No, I was watching Discovery…'

'Well, switch over to Preda and we'll talk afterwards.'

Preda's chat show featured Nenișor Vasile in a near apoplectic state, face to face with an apparently calm Commander Movil?, Head of the Bucharest Police. The Minister wondered how Movil? had made the decision to appear on the show without consulting him first, but he tried not to get upset before hearing what Nenişor had to say.

'Mr Movil?, this is the tenth time I'm asking you ... isn't it, Mr Preda?'

'Asking him what, sir? You've asked a lot of questions...'

'I've asked over and over. When are you going to catch this criminal? How many more people need to die before you do your duty properly? Tell me exactly how many people are working on this case! Zero, I presume? My sources tell me that your minister has refused to allocate any more resources to the investigation. To hell with the gypsies, he said, there are far too many of them anyway! Because, if he had given you even one extra person – a child, an intern, a half-blind retired officer, you'd have still been able to find a clue. But no, you have nothing at all. Is it because you're incurably stupid? Certainly not! Because if it had been about a gypsy stealing a loaf of bread, you'd have arrested him in less than a day. You'd have sent a hundred officers to arrest him and maybe even shot two innocent bystanders in the process...'

Movil?'s face was turning crimson too by now. 'Mr Preda, do you still need me here, or are you just going to give free rein to the deputy here to swear at the police and the Ministry of the Interior?'

'You know that we practice freedom of speech here, as an independent TV station. So Mr Vasile is free to say what he pleases, as are you.'

'Speaking of which,' Nenişor interrupted, 'In today's programme on another TV station, which clearly is more biased towards the government, that sourpuss Irina Lascar...'

'Please don't insult other TV stations on my show, sir...'

'Why shouldn't I? Is it a free country or not? Or have they bought you as well?'

It was Preda's turn now to turn red. 'Excuse me, sir. This is my show, on a private TV channel, and the only things which can hold us to account are the laws of the country and our audience. Nobody is buying or selling me, I'm not a potato. The National Audiovisual Council forbids me to attack other TV stations, regardless of any personal opinions I might hold about the quality of their programmes or their presenters. So I do not allow anyone to criticise any journalist, is that clear? If you ever want to appear again on this channel, I would advise you bear that in mind. And now, Commander...'

Nenişor did not give up easily, but he tried to pacify his host. 'I'm sorry, please don't get cross, Mr Preda.'

'It's the Commander's opportunity to speak now. You can present your point of view afterwards.'

'I would like to state, firstly, that I cannot mention anything relating to the investigation, because any detail could be useful to the killer,' Movilă said. 'And, secondly, it's classified information, so I cannot tell you how many people are working on the case, but I can assure there are plenty.'

'Well, in that case, you're all idiots! Maybe we should handle the investigation ourselves.'

'Who's we? The MPs?'

'Us gypsies, General – or Chief Constable or whatever you are calling yourself now. And, when we catch him, you will see that he was one of yours...'

'One of ours?'

'A policeman or someone with a connection the police. That's why you're incapable of catching him. You're all in it together. You seem to be so much more on the ball when you're chasing some poor gypsy bastard who's stolen a loaf of bread.'

Preda had to intervene again, to allow Movilă to speak.

'I have to admit, I'm not sure if Mr Vasile's words are guided by malevolence or sheer stupidity...'

Nenișor Vasile was ready to go for the jugular again, but Preda stopped him with a look. At least, for the time being.

'The poor gypsy bastard that Mr Vasile is referring to, the ones we go after with our special forces, most frequently is a member of criminal gangs, notorious not just in Romania but also abroad. When arresting those so-called poor bastards who steal a loaf of bread, what tends to happen is that they suddenly produce automatic rifles and shoot policemen. Regarding the Sword case, I can reassure viewers that we are on the killer's trail, but our job is more about action rather than about throwing words around irresponsibly.'

'What about that irresponsible statement that the killer is a gypsy himself?'

'I don't know anything about that.'

Come on, General. On that TV station that I'm not allowed to mention because Mr Preda will get cross with me, this guy appeared and said that the assassin was a gypsy. What's that all about?'

'I repeat: I don't know anything about that.'

Preda announced that they had Laurenţiu Petre on the line, the psychologist who had stated that the killer was a gypsy.

'So tell us, Mr Petre. Who gave you instructions to lie about the killer? Who is your paymaster?'

'Can I just say that I didn't state that the killer is a gypsy. All I said was that he could be and gave a few examples from the research. I am a specialist in forensic psychology and completed a Ph.D. on the subject of serial killers in the US. I studied behavioural psychology for four years at Quantico. And I now work in the Romanian Information Services.'

'There you go, I told you he was pro-government.'

'I'm not pro-anyone. Yesterday in Parliament, you mentioned that you had a Ph.D. in Science. I respect your qualifications, so why don't you respect mine? You are doing your ethnicity a disservice if you keep on attacking all the public institutions of the Romanian state. And you're doing them a disservice if you keep threatening with reprisals and acts of revenge. As far as the killer goes, Mr Movil?'s position is absolutely correct: until the killer is caught, there is no point in speculating... I just put forward a hypothesis.'

'All right, I admit I lost my temper. I don't believe that the killer is from my community. I think it's far more likely that he is a policeman. But let me warn you ... if you don't catch the killer sharpish, there will be problems. And the flames aren't being fanned by me or by the Union of the Romas. The Roma soul will suffer in silence for decades and decades, but at some point they reach breaking point.'

'That sounds like a threat again,' said Movil?.

'Not a threat at all,' Nenişor was unusually calm now. 'Merely a warning. Catch him as fast as you can and that's it. The dead remain dead, unfortunately, but at least the living can get on with their lives. Right now, the dead and the living are getting all mixed up. That's dangerous.'

13

At three in the morning, a thunderstorm broke over Bucharest. It was payback after the endless row of hot days. At first no more than a few minutes of menacing growls of thunder, then it started raining heavily. By six that morning, when the commuters came out, the streets were flooded and the rain still showed no signs of letting up. A few unlucky drivers, barefoot, with their trousers rolled up, were trying to push their cars out of the puddles as large as ponds which had engulfed some of the lower-lying junctions.

The lorry carrying the coffins of Sile the Butcher and Costi was surrounded by people who wanted to accompany them to the cemetery. Two thousand people had initially said they would take part, but the rain and poor communications had reduced the numbers to no more than two hundred and fifty. The funeral procession had started on Liberty Boulevard, then continued on Liviu Rebreanu Street and through the block of flats towards the cemetery. Nenișor Vasile marched just a few paces behind the convoy, alongside Iliescu, the VP of the Romanian Foundation for the Protection of Human Rights, the President of the

League for the Protection of Ethnic Minorities and an American journalist sent to Bucharest by Amnesty International.

The convoy was surrounded by a police cordon, while two anti-terrorist jeeps followed discreetly behind. They'd been expecting a few leaders of the criminal gangs to show up, but neither Costi nor Sile the Butcher were important enough, so no-one was present. That didn't deter reporters and cameramen, at least forty of them, who had gathered to watch the procession advancing down Murgului Way, alongside the wall of the cemetery.

Suddenly, from the block of flats opposite, they heard loud booing and whistling. All the cameras turned in that direction. A group of people were shouting at the convoy from the top two floors. An old man waved his walking stick angrily at the mourners, but when the reporters tried to approach him to hear what he was saying, he disappeared inside.

There was more shouting coming from another block of flats, across several floors. A gaggle of youngsters had huddled together in the anaemic green space between the blocks of flats and were apparently saluting the convoy. Then they made throat-slitting gestures instead. One of them wore a T shirt with a picture of a blood-drenched dagger. Drops of blood spelled out the word SWORD.

Two Romas from the convoy were ready to start trading blows with the youngsters, but a policeman moved them on. Major Costache was supervising the convoy and realised that the shit was about to hit the fan. He requested back-up, knowing that two more police vans were on standby nearby. He ordered three policemen to disperse the young people, which they did without further ado.

Suddenly, an object came flying at them from one of the windows. A jar full of liquid. The jar smashed against the lorry, sending liquid and shards flying towards those nearest to the lorry. One of the Romas who was perched on the back of the lorry dipped a finger in the liquid, sniffed it and let the others know it was urine.

What came next caught everyone by surprise. Two dozen Romas broke through the police cordon all of a sudden and rushed towards the building from where the jar had been launched. Chaos ensued, as some of the policemen tried to re-establish the cordon, while others chased after the furious Romas. One of the men shouted that he was sure that the jar had been thrown from the second floor. The police managed to restrain most of those trying to enter the building, but four Romas evaded them and rushed up the stairs. One old man had been trampled underfoot and was lying on the floor, crying for help, but no-one dared to open the door.

The four who reached the second floor started hammering and kicking at the door, until it came off its hinges, together with part of the plastered wall. The hallway was dark and empty. They ran into the kitchen. No-one there. Nor in the pantry. No-one in the living room, either; one of them even went out on the balcony to check. The door from the living room to the second little hallway leading to the bedrooms and bathroom was locked. They tried once more to kick it in, but by then four burly policemen, equipped with balaclavas and truncheons, had caught up with them. They were told to lie down, were handcuffed and taken away from there.

Major Costache knocked on the locked door.

'This is the police. Open up!'

Not a sound. He knocked again, but there was no answer. He got two of his officers to break down the door. In the bedroom they found two young lads, sixteen and twelve years old. They were rigid with fear and crying. They'd been the ones who'd thrown the jar, because the gypsies were throwing their weight around in their neighbourhood. They'd been bullied and beaten up, their bikes had been stolen. So Sword was doing a good job, right? Major Costache felt like slapping them, but he managed to restrain himself and just swore at them instead. He told them to call their parents at once. He left a few policemen in the flat and went back downstairs, where things had calmed down a little.

The funeral procession had reached the cemetery now. It was packed with policemen, anti-terrorist units and security guards. The old man who'd been trampled in the doorway was on his way to hospital, but seemed to have suffered only a few minor cuts. The four Romas were taken away to the police station.

The clouds lifted and the sun was starting to dry out the puddles. It was going to be a beautiful September morning.

14

The main opposition party called a press conference, organised as usual by their leader Radu Rădulescu, on course to become the next president if his party won the elections. Opinion polls already had him ahead of the incumbent president, and there were still more than twelve months until the next elections. The topic for the press conference had initially been advertised as a protest against the revised budget, which the government had been working on during the parliamentary recess over the summer. But Rădulescu had changed the agenda and was instead reading out a statement regarding his party's position about the unfortunate recent incidents at the cemetery.

'Our party is concerned, as is the vast majority of the general public, that the living standards in Romania are falling and that poverty is on the increase. In the past three years poverty levels have risen across all strata of society, which has led to a series of consequences that make life difficult for the average Romanian. I am talking about a rise in violence in our cities, higher crime rates, interethnic and interreligious intolerance and hatred. The current government has shown itself to be incapable of resolving these issues.

'The parties in the current governing coalition made it very clear in their election campaign three years ago that they would eliminate such anti-social behaviour. But that has turned out to be just one more broken promise. Our households are poorer and our streets far less secure. The latest in a long list of government failures is the case known as the Sword killings. It's been over a month now that the inhabitants of our capital city have been terrorised by the unpredictable acts of a killer or group of killers. The police has been helpless; their incompetence yesterday led to a violent confrontation between frightened citizens, who feel unsure and abandoned. If the Sword case is not resolved as soon as possible, we will take all political measures necessary to resolve this dilemma. We may even ask for a motion of no confidence in the President, since he is the supreme military commander in this country, and therefore has clear responsibilities in this area. I ought to remind our head of state that Article 80, paragraph 2 of the Romanian Constitution states that: "The President of Romania ensures that the Constitution is respected by all, and that the public institutions are functioning properly. The President is therefore a mediator between the different powers in the state, and between the state and the society."

'Our current President has been very keen to raise his profile as a regional leader, but he needs to understand that he not only represents his country abroad, but that he is above all the President of all Romanian citizens, including the eight who have been killed over the last month. We therefore advise him to take a direct interest in the way in which his Cabinet, and in particular the Minister of the Interior, are handling this case.'

Radu Rădulescu put down his papers, took off his glasses, and asked the journalists gathered around him if they had any further questions. If not, they could return to the planned agenda for the day. A British radio journalist, notorious for his rather acerbic comments about the opposition, stood up.

'Mr Rădulescu, what is your relationship with Mr Nenişor Vasile, the representative for the Roma minority in parliament?'

'Mr Vasile is a well-respected member of the Romanian cultural community. I have also personally met his father and I cannot help but think that it would be great if all members of the Roma community were as exemplary as this family.'

'Mr Vasile predicted in parliament that this whole thing could degenerate into a war between Romanians and Romas. Is that a likely scenario, given what happened yesterday in front of the cemetery at Izvorul Tămăduirii?'

'If you have any questions about Mr Vasile's statements, then I suggest you ask him directly. However, I deeply regret the escalation of conflict between the different ethnic groups and I hold the government responsible for that.'

'Is it true that Mr Vasile is likely to be one of your candidates at the next election?' the British journalist continued unperturbed.

'I have no idea if he will be a candidate or not, and I don't see how this question is relevant. This is not a problem created by Mr Vasile or my party. The problem has been created by this criminal, while you the press have been eager to bestow a memorable nickname upon him, and the police seem incapable of catching him. Any other questions?'

A journalist from a private TV channel got up next.

'When you say you might attempt a motion of no confidence, you are undoubtedly aware that the President has a majority in parliament. Where do you think you will find the two thirds of votes necessary to remove him?'

'I refuse to believe that our MPs are mere voting robots, who go mindlessly with whatever their party tells them. I'm sure that in an emergency such as this one, they will remember that their first duty is towards the electorate.'

'You'll have heard the hypothesis that the killer could be a Roma. Would you like to comment on this? Or is it fake news being spread by the government?'

'I have no desire to speculate about such matters. I have no idea who the murderer is. In fact, that's the crux of the problem. We do not know the identity of the murderer, so rumours are flying around wildly. Everyone's got an opinion, including the police. Let's catch him first, then we can see whether he is a Roma or not.'

Tom Evans, the American journalist who had accompanied the funeral procession, stood up.

'On the way to the cemetery, I saw Romanian youths behaving in a highly irresponsible fashion, provoking the Romas. I saw an old man trampled underfoot, and two kids throwing a bottle of urine at the coffins. I saw such hatred in their faces, hatred against those of another race. I'm a war correspondent and I've been to Bosnia, Nagorno-Karabakh, Somalia and most recently Kosovo. It's the same hatred wherever I go. Isn't that the real issue at stake here, not the killer or the President, but the hatred between Romanians and Romas?'

Radu Rădulescu smiled broadly and took off his glasses. Nodding gently, he replied to the American journalist directly in English.

'Mr Evans, we are very tolerant people. We don't have ethnic problems, we love each other. Romania is not like Kosovo, or like Bosnia. Believe me, we are a completely different kind of nation. We've never had ethnic conflict in our country. Ask the Romanian people. You will see that the number one concern for 66% of them is the way this government is handling things in this country. And if you ask them tomorrow, that percentage may well be higher. But fear not, we'll change the government next year and all of these problems will cease.'

15

Three years ago we had a long drought – one of the worst droughts in the last hundred years or so. There was no rain for months, the crops were blighted, we were expecting food shortages. The main opposition party blamed the drought on the President.

Two years ago, with our typical luck in such matters, we suffered from flooding. Houses lost in landslides, people left destitute, a few dead, crops destroyed once more. The same opposition party blamed the rain and the disaster once more on the government and the President. Especially the President.

Last year, we had severe winter weather. It started snowing in October and didn't stop until April. Roads blocked, people snowed in, all sorts of problems. And who was to blame? You've guessed it – the President, of course!

This year there's been no drought, no flooding, and we still have a way to go before the winter sets in. What we do have this year is a serial killer who has already claimed the lives of eight people. If you read the press release of the opposition party – and bear in mind that these words reflect the opinions of their candidate for next year's presidential elections, Radu Rădulescu – you will find that the blame lies once more with the government and the President. I fear that what it shows us is that Mr Rădulescu is far too obsessed with becoming president himself once more.

Let's not forget that when he was leading the country, there were just as many floods, droughts and blizzards. There were also plenty of crimes – many of them committed by his closest allies. There were plenty of economic failures and instances of being isolated as a country politically. That is why Mr Rădulescu and his party lost the election a few years back. However, if he does ever become president again, I'm sure that Mr Rădulescu would not want to be blamed for all the bad things that are happening in Romania. So this tendency of his to destabilise the party in power at all costs, even at the risk of interethnic conflict, contradicts his stated intentions of patriotism and acting responsibly. When the internal stability of Romania is at stake, all political parties should work together. If Mr Rădulescu cannot understand and accept that, then maybe he shouldn't be a candidate for the presidential palace at Cotroceni.

Mircică reread his editorial with some trepidation. In the last fifteen minutes he'd received one phone call after another, both from the President's security adviser and from the opposition party secretary. Neither of them liked his editorial. The Cotroceni spokesperson warned him that they would terminate his paper's advertising contracts with the Tobacco Consortium and the Privatisation Agency, as well as stop the funding he was currently receiving from a private bank headquartered in Transylvania. Meanwhile, Rădulescu's guy was threatening him that he would be the first casualty once they won the election.

The President was furious because the editorial played with the possibility that Rădulescu might become president once again. Plus, he felt that Mircică was far too gentle with the opposition.

'Have you heard Ionescu or Cârstea being that amiable towards them? Why on earth are you so soft with Rădulescu? Do you honestly think he won't punish you if he ever gets into power? We had an understanding that you were going to mention two specific cases of criminal corruption involving Rădulescu's men. Why didn't you?'

Thus the President's security adviser, excelling in his usual acrimonious tone and invective. Mircică tried to explain that there would be a much more detailed follow-up article, but the adviser told him it was probably too late. The President was in talks with another journalist, who would be prepared to collaborate more closely with him.

The opposition party secretary was an old friend of Mircică's, back in the days when they both got on with Rădulescu, when their party was in power. He was equally harsh, telling Mircică that his boss viewed this as a personal betrayal, and that his entire attitude over the past three years was unforgivable.

'You know full well who helped you set up the paper, and who turned you into a respectable journalist from the two-bit scruff of a hack you used to be. Don't forget who made you a member of all those press committees and granted you the import licence for paper, the first ever granted in Romania! Yes, we understand that you need to make a living even after we lost the elections, but plenty of others have done so with a bit more decency than you have. We all have to compromise, but you're really taking the piss. My boss asked me to tell you that he won't forget this, and he will get his revenge once he is re-elected. As for me, I want to tell you that you are a senile piece of shit and it will be my pleasure to take you down. Now run off to Cotroceni and whine about mistreatment!'

16

Sergiu Enescu was approaching his 80th birthday, but he was still by far the most respected political analyst. His TV programmes always had a huge audience, and his predictions often influenced political leaders. It's true that not all of his predictions turned out to be correct, but there was no-one to analyse the data. Everyone wanted a piece of him, so he usually chose to help the party in power and the most promising opposition parties. It had been unexpectedly difficult to win the trust of the current President, who had resisted hiring him because of his previous cosy relationship with Radu Rădulescu. After a year or so, the icy relationship finally thawed and there were now invitations to Cotroceni on a more or less monthly basis. The President seemed to really appreciate his advice.

He was shown, as usual, into the silverware reception room. A bodyguard brought him a cup of tea, some biscuits and a selection of papers. That meant the President was going to be running late. He glanced at the headlines, munched two biscuits and fell asleep in the comfortable armchair set in the warm sunlight. He was woken up when the President opened the door.

'I'm sorry, Mr Enescu, but there's so much to prepare for the French President's visit next week. If only I could do everything myself. But I can't, and nobody else seems capable of doing things properly without my supervision. I keep getting called in to soothe ruffled feathers and repair relationships, get my men to work together properly… They're right in a way – nobody is ever grateful, nobody ever thanks them or appreciates their hard work. And they do work hard. Maybe not always terribly efficiently, but they do work long hours. It must seem so unfair to them that I'll be the one to go down in the history books, while they'll simply go silently to their graves. Excuse me just one more second.'

The President left the room once more. Enescu had barely got the gist of the President's monologue, because he'd only just woken up and was still quite disoriented. He shifted in the armchair and tried to recall if the President had said anything important. In the meantime, the man in question whizzed back into the room together with a bodyguard bringing more biscuits and tea.

'If you don't mind, I'll eat while we talk. Never have time otherwise. So, what do you think of this whole Sword business?'

'Well, sir…' Enescu was about to start, but the President interrupted him.

'Isn't it crazy how much Ionescu, Cârstea and the others hate my guts? Putting me on a par with this murderer! Here I am preparing for an important visit by the President of France, then I'm heading off to speak at the NATO conference. I'll see the German Chancellor there and ask for her support. Then we have the largest ever delegation of Japanese businessmen coming to see us. All of this is happening within the next month or so, and that's before we even get to the OSCE Summit we're hosting later. But nobody sees all of this. Nobody mentions the fact that I've introduced reforms, that we finally have a booming economy, that there is no more corruption in the banking sector, that we've privatised more in one year than any of our predecessors in five years. No, all they want to talk about is the serial killer. And I'm to blame for his very existence. What am I supposed to do – catch him myself?'

'Of course not, Mr President, but someone has to catch him. Otherwise you run the risk that all of your internal and external achievements will be overshadowed by this phenomenon.'

'What do you mean?'

'Well, if it had been a common serial killer, choosing his victims at random, that would have been less serious, but this one kills only gypsies.'

'You're right. We've already had some international organisations breathing down our necks. The Danish and Swedish ambassadors have been asked to present a report to their respective governments. The EU will give us grief if…'

'I wasn't referring to those kinds of problems. I was trying to say that if the victims had been entirely random, everyone would have been shocked. However, given that the victims are gypsies and criminals, there is a certain sector of society which tacitly approves of the killer's actions. I've been following the incident at the cemetery closely and it seems to me that the majority Romanian population could act in a way that could trigger the Roma minority … and that could lead to all sorts of interethnic violence.'

'I disagree. All of this has been blown up by the press and MPs like Nenişor. And of course, my old mate Radu Rădulescu, who is so keen to be back in power that he's ready to step over dead bodies to get there! There are serial killers everywhere in the world, there've been entire volumes written about them – but I don't see any other country blaming their leader for the actions of a psychopath? And you know what, Mr Enescu, you too are to blame in all of this. If you'd taken a firm position when they first came out with those threats of civil war and whatnot, then they'd have stopped writing all that nonsense. You all tell me how much you'll help me during the election campaign … but I need your help now. This is when the elections get decided. I'm meeting the French President, but it's Rădulescu who goes up in the opinion polls because some madman is murdering gypsies in Bucharest. You could, for example, give Rădulescu a low score in your Sunday programme.'

'What for?'

'For raising the whole gypsy issue and proposing a vote of no-confidence against me.'

'And should I also give the Minister of the Interior a low rating for not catching the murderer?'

'Yes. But Rădulescu should have the lowest score. Three for him and five for the Minister. Someone should also point out how similar and incendiary Rădulescu's words are to Slobodan Milošević's, who dragged his country into civil war. And you should point out that there's a difference between a politician and a statesman. A politician will do everything for the sake of his party, but a statesman does what is best for his country. He is above petty ideologies and group interests. He can plan many years ahead, and see what is truly for the good of the country, even when others do not share his vision. You know full well I could have taken the easy route, the nationalist-populist route, without embarking on any reforms, and not move this country towards NATO and EU membership. I'm sure the polls would have rewarded me for that.'

'I don't think you need to worry about the next election, sir. But your team has made some mistakes regarding this case. The murderer needs to be caught and condemned as soon as possible. And all the attacks against you will suddenly turn into something really positive. If they associate you so closely with this case, then obviously you will get the credit for catching the criminal. I suggest a public appearance, in which you deplore the sorry state of affairs that took place at the cemetery, and you make an appeal for calm and maturity. Then send a strong message to the police that you expect them to do everything in their power to catch the killer or else there will be severe consequences. When he does get caught, people will appreciate it was because of your firm attitude. People want a show of strength.'

The President sat back in his chair. He looked tired, old and frail. He stared into the distance for a short while, then admitted that the police had no leads at all in the Sword case.

'Not a single clue. Nothing. This guy is a professional, possibly a former policeman, because he really knows how to hide any traces. He could strike at any time, anywhere, maybe even go beyond Bucharest. There are three million gypsies in Romania, several hundred thousand of these have criminal records. So many potential victims – we can't protect them all. The police are working their butts off. Next week we've got someone from the FBI showing up. And Interpol is already helping.'

17

The Minister of the Interior had been waiting for ten minutes. He knew what to expect, however. Andrei Rusu was never less than twenty minutes late and would invariably show up nattering away to a VIP on his mobile. Then there would be the usual ritual of patching four or five of his team members into their conversation via a conference call, and it would all end with him giving them a long list of things to do, including the Minister himself. But it was a price worth paying, because Rusu was the Director General of the most powerful TV channel in Romania.

Bucharest looked woebegone and grey through the floor-to-ceiling windows. It was raining heavily. Rusu's PA let the Minister know that her boss was about to arrive. There were two rows of TV monitors showing all the news channels from Romania, plus CNN and Euronews. The Minister was about to try and turn up the sound so he could hear a round-up of the sports on Euronews, when Rusu arrived, talking on the phone of course. He kept him waiting for another five minutes, then organised a hasty teleconference on the subject of the French President's state visit. He barked some orders, asked the Minister to share his views on the topic with the participants on the call, then arranged a weekend meeting with the President's security adviser at his villa in Snagov. Finally, he turned to the Minister and proclaimed that he was all ears. The Minister did not beat around the bush, bored as he was of all the waiting:

'In his show yesterday, Enescu scored me a five because I haven't been able to catch the gypsy killer.'

'So I heard.'

'Look, it's your business if you want to keep that senile old man on your channel, but I thought our relationship deserved better than that.'

'You know who told him to give you a five? I asked him. It was the President himself, last week.'

'But you know who's behind it all, don't you? It's your dear friend whom you are meeting in Snagov this coming weekend.'

'Hold your horses, the President doesn't care much for you much either. They're all baying for your blood and you've given them the perfect excuse. Speaking of which, are you any closer to catching the killer?'

'Leave it! I want to know what you're going to do about Enescu!'

Rusu quickly set up another teleconference.

'Listen up, everyone. I've got the Minister of the Interior here with me. We want to organise a week-long special about fighting crime. So I want something general, but also specific stories. I want teams sent to all parts of the country to film police interventions, night-time filming, armed raids, arresting criminals, interviews with people who are happy that the perpetrators have been caught and so on. I also want a major talk show with the Minister, demonstrating what a committed crimebuster he is. We can do some research on… never mind, drop it, not yet! Every news bulletin should have a special feature dedicated to this, some human interest story. Come up with some other ideas too! Tomorrow I want to meet you all at 22:07 and finalise all the details. Thanks and goodbye. Dana, please stay on the line.'

After everyone else had hung up, Rusu gave his PA instructions.

'Talk to Enescu. On his next show, I want the Minister to be his 'Man of the Week.' And send me that research report on crime figures.'

He hung up and winked at the Minister. 'Happy now?'

'I'm not sure what you mean by armed raids…'

'Arrange for a few showy scenes like that, so my guys have something juicy to film. Get the special forces guys in masks out, arrest a few slowcoaches and leave the PR to us. No big deal. Oh, and I suggest giving it a catchy title. Something like "Mission Clean-Up". Admittedly, that sounds a bit sinister, but find a suitable title, OK? I'll have one of my guys call you and you can tell him where to catch you all in action. And now tell me about Sword? Are you any closer to catching him?'

'I'll be perfectly honest with you. You may have noticed that I've got police cars on every corner, at every intersection.'

'Yes, good move that!'

'Not really – the reason they're all there is because I don't have sufficient petrol to move them around. The criminals we're trying to catch have monster BMWs or Mercs, while we have Dacias with twenty litres in the tank. Last week, a gang started shooting at my men with Uzis, right next to the border with Bulgaria. Meanwhile, we have to give them due warning, shoot in the air and only then fire at them. Many of the mafia gangs have recruited some of our best policemen or assault troops, who can each handle ten or fifteen rookie cops in one go. Every petty criminal has found himself a former police officer or a retired anti-corruption brigade officer who can advise him how to avoid getting caught. And then of course there's corruption at the highest level, even I am not fully aware how much. So that's the background before we even get to the Sword scenario.

'What is strange about this case is that, for the most part, organised crime gangs in Romania generally try to avoid killing anyone. Most violent crime here is domestic, drunken brawls, jealousy, fighting over money... There are very few professional hits. But if the local gangs start getting ideas above their station, then we might end up with ten Swords per year. And we are simply not ready to deal with that. Sword knows the rules all too well and he's careful to cover his traces, leave nothing to chance. Our foreign experts agree that he's either an ex-policeman or has someone to advise him. And you might have noticed that he doesn't crave any publicity. No puzzles or messages sent to the police, nothing. This guy doesn't want to get caught, doesn't want to be famous, and if he stops killing tomorrow it's very likely that we'll never catch him.'

'In other words, you have nothing…'

'Very little. He hasn't put a foot wrong so far. All we know is that he's choosing gypsies with criminal records, and he kills them with a single blow to the neck.'

'Except for the guy with his head in the bag…'

'That wasn't him. That was one of those rare instances of a revenge killing and it was his mistress who betrayed him. We caught her three days ago about to board a ship in Constanța and she helped us identify the killers. Palestinians. They've left the country but we've got Interpol tracking them. No, our guy kills with a single blow to the front of the throat. Our forensic specialists are convinced that it's a single killer – he's got a certain technique. But of course, he could have a group of people helping him cover up the traces.'

Rusu's PA came in with a blue folder with a Post-it note attached.

'Ah, here's the report I asked my social researchers to prepare. I picked a representative sample of 1500 viewers from across the country and asked them what they thought of the Sword case. Fifty per cent didn't know or hadn't heard of it, although that was before the cemetery incident. I'm sure the figures have changed since then. The remaining fifty per cent are divided. Half of them are against the killer, but half of them think he is doing a good job bringing about social justice. So… if you keep on delaying things, you might not even want to announce that you've caught the perpetrator, because by then public opinion might have swung against you! Anyway, we thought of announcing next week that we're offering a reward for anyone who helps us catch the assassin. A billion lei in the old currency – hundred thousand new lei – for anyone who has significant information leading to his arrest. That might help you…'

'But if you're planning to film those raids and so on, then don't offer a reward to the public at the same time, or you'll make me look incompetent. First make me look good and then offer the reward.'

'Fine then. Now, I need your help to sweeten that guy from the Privatisation Fund…'

18

Tony had his earpiece in and was quietly awaiting his turn. First a sports update, a football coach who'd been fired and was now taking his employers to court, then some adverts for condoms, mobile phones and an anti-ageing cream, and then finally the theme tune for his show.

'Good evening, here's the latest from Intrepid Tony. Summer is over, September is nearly over, schools have started, but instead of counting new pupils, we're counting dead bodies. We've got eight at present – some people say even nine. The press is having a fit, the opposition is having a fit, the President is having a fit about why the press and the opposition are frothing at the mouth about him, and the police sees no evil, hears no evil, catches no evil. It would be fair to say that things are somewhat complicated and secretive. So of course Intrepid Tony is on the case – because Intrepid is my middle name, right?

'In case you missed it, tonight's programme will be all about this Sword guy who goes around eviscerating gypsies – sorry, I mean Rrroma – with however many Rs you want to write it. Give us a call and tell us what you think about this matter. Some people consider the armed guy to be a kind of hero, punishing those whom the judges and prosecutors are incapable of punishing, because they're up to their elbows in bribes from the criminals. Others say he is a maniac who must be caught as soon as possible. Some even go so far as to claim that he must be a policeman. So far, he hasn't touched anyone except Romas with a criminal record. Is that a good thing or a bad thing? Would these delinquents be stopped otherwise? Does democracy mean that we have to treat criminals with kid gloves because of their human rights? As if they care about anyone else's human rights! I may not agree with the Chinese government, but there's something to be said for executing criminals in stadiums. If you know that you might get a bullet to your head, you're less likely to get involved in a life of crime.

'And here is our first caller. Good evening, what's your name?'

'Hello, I'm Alina and I'm calling from Bucharest.'

'I don't want to appear overly curious, but are you a gypsy by any chance?'

'No, I'm not, but I have to say that I find your remarks about them deeply offensive. How can you condone such a murderer?'

'Offensive… condone… nice words. Alina, my dear, are you a student by any chance?'

'I was once. I'm a sociologist now and I'd just like to say that you and others like you are stirring up hatred which could lead to a real social time bomb that will scar us all.'

'Ah, so you're a gypsy lover, are you? Pardon me, I mean Rroma, of course... Now imagine that you're a young lady who has come to Bucharest for work. You come from a godforsaken little town in Moldova that had a single factory built by Ceaușescu, which then shut down after Ceaușescu got shot. And the whole town shut down with it. Your dad's unemployed and has started drinking heavily. Your mum's unemployed too. You've just finished your technical school and decide to go to Bucharest to try and find work there. You arrive at night at the main railway station because the train connections are terrible, and this slimy guy starts picking on you. You turn him down, so he follows you and forces you at knife-point into his van. He takes you to a run-down house in the slums and for all of the following week he rapes you, alongside three or four of his mates. Then he moves you to another slum, where he pimps you out at an hourly rate. Thirty, forty men later... Have you even known that many men, Alina?'

'This has nothing to do with...'

'You're right. But just imagine if you were this young lass – what would you like to do to this guy who has shown you such a good time in a mere few weeks?'

'The justice system should...'

'Pah, have you never heard of corrupt judges? What power does a nineteen-year-old girl from a godforsaken dump in Moldova have against the deep pockets of the smartarse who shows up in his fancy Mercedes with three lawyers who are on a first name basis with the judge? Maybe he gets seven years in prison – you weren't a minor after all. And with a spot of good behaviour, he'll be out in three. Meanwhile, your life has been destroyed. Never mind the fact that the guy might be a trifle upset that you turned him in, so he and his mates will come looking for you…'

'I think you are using an extreme scenario to get people on your side…'

'My dear Alina, this scenario is real. The guy in question is none other than Sword's third victim. His name was Savoiu, known as Fane the Slut, and he was a pimp. He'd been imprisoned twice but he continued to ply his trade. I personally interviewed this poor girl for three hours and she told me stories you just wouldn't believe. Stories about this guy and his mates, none of whom ever got more than a slap on the wrist. You see, my dear, the justice system is for honest people like yourself. It doesn't scare people like them at all. Because they've learnt to play it.'

'So what are you suggesting? That we go back to the Middle Ages? An eye for an eye, a tooth for a tooth?'

'You never answered my question. I want an honest answer from you. What would you have liked to do to this Slut guy if you'd been in this wretched girl's place?'

'Well, you're never going to get me to say that I wanted him dead. Because I think that only God has the right to take life.'

'Amen to that. God has the right to take life, and Fane the Slut has the right to take your virginity. Thanks for your call. Let's go over to Line 2, where we have someone who's been waiting patiently for quite a while. Good evening, sorry to have kept you waiting…'

'Evening.'

'And you are…'

'I'm Alexander from Bucharest and I'd like to say that if all you said about that poor girl is true, then he deserved a fate far worse than death…'

'I'm afraid the girl's story is true.'

'I think it's all the gypsies' fault. They refuse to work, they've got accustomed to stealing and because of them all of Europe hates us. Everywhere you go abroad, they point at you and consider you a gypsy, because Roma and Romanian sound so similar.'

'I see… So, what is your opinion about this Sword guy?'

'I think he's doing a good job. Clearly, the gypsies have bought the police and the judges, so they can do whatever they damn well please in this country. If there were more Swords throughout the country, just you wait and see how their criminal behaviour might change…'

'Fine, thank you, Alexander. Over to the other line. Good evening, what's your name?'

'I am Andrei Gabriel Iliescu and I'm the Vice President of the Romanian Foundation for the Protection of Human Rights. I'd just like to tell you that I am recording this show and will send it – with a translation – to all European organisations for the protection of minority rights, because you are actually inciting people to commit hate crimes. I will also contact the National Audiovisual Council and ask them to stop this show at once and to fine your radio station for it. That's all. Good night.'

'Don't you want to hear my point of view, Mr Iliescu…? He hung up. Well, my dear listeners, now that you know this is being recorded and that the whole Council of Europe will hear you, please feel free to call in. Sure enough, we've got somebody eager to voice their opinion on Line 1. Good evening.'

'My name is Octavian, calling from Ploieşti, and I'd like to tell you that I respect your courage, but Sword's solution is definitely not the right one. Regardless how many problems the gypsies cause – and I agree they cause a lot of them – you can't just kill whomever you like.'

'What do you think of Mr Iliescu's threat to expose us in Europe?'

'He's an idiot if he thinks that you can forbid anything in Romania currently. As for Europe – if they're so keen on the gypsies, why do they keep sending them back home to us? They're even more racist than we are.'

'Are you saying I shouldn't stop this show for fear they might monitor us at the Council of Europe?'

'Not at all. If they keep sending the gypsies back, then they should at least let us talk about them as we please.'

'Thank you, Octavian. Another caller… What's your name and are you scared of the Council of Europe?'

'My name isn't important.'

'Shall I call you Shy Boy then? What's your opinion of Sword? Is he doing something good or bad?'

'That doesn't matter. The question is, will he strike again?'

'And what do you think? Will he?'

'I think the police should search carefully in one of the forests around Bucharest.'

'What for?'

'What do you think, Intrepid Tony? For crows. It's crow season ... especially in the forest.'

'Shy Boy, is there something you're not telling us?'

'I just told you.'

'Do you have information about Sword?'

'I didn't say that.'

'Or are you Sword?'

'Maybe I am. But you do jump to conclusions, don't you? Bye.'

'Wait, don't hang up! Dammit! Well, ladies and gentlemen, if I'm not mistaken, we might just have had the most wanted person in Romania on the line. We'll be back after a short break.'

19

The next day, Stoicescu, Head of the Intelligence Services, skimmed through the report he'd received about the controversial radio show. Tony and his producer had been questioned intensely that morning and had admitted that it was all a prank. The caller who had pretended to be Sword was in fact an employee of the radio station, who was often tasked with making the shows 'livelier'. But, to be fair, he hadn't actually claimed to be Sword, nor did he say exactly what might be found in the forests surrounding Bucharest.

Stoicescu's PA stuck her head through the door and said, softly (there was nothing her boss hated more than strident tones): 'The President for you on the red line...'

'Well, have you caught him, Stoicescu?'

'I'm afraid not, sir. It was a prank from the radio guys.'

'A prank?'

'Yes, to boost their listener numbers. The caller was one of their own.'

'Close down that radio station immediately.'

'We can't do that, sir.'

'But they lied to us, they tried to trick us. I had a press conference prepared and ... what do I do now?'

'That's not the major problem, sir. The problem is we've found a new body in the Andronache forest. Killed in exactly the same way as the previous eight. He must have been dead for a while – possibly the sixth victim in chronological order.'

'And he's a gypsy too?'

'It would seem so, although we haven't identified him yet.'

'So how did that silly prank lead to a new body?'

'We are questioning them right now. It would appear to be an unfortunate coincidence. But we'll have a hard job convincing the press. The last thing we need now is for them to spread rumours that we actually know who the killer is, that we've caught him but are keeping it secret.'

'This is utterly absurd.'

'We'll blame the radio station. We'll get the presenter, the producer and the prankster to hold a press conference and explain everything.'

'But you refuse to shut down the radio station...'

'Legally, we're not allowed to do that. I've got the audio transcript for the show and no one ever claimed that it was the voice of the murderer. Admittedly, you could argue that the presenter was deliberately racist, anti-gypsy, inciting hatred. We could revoke their licence. But there were enough people troubled by the idea of young girls being raped, so it wouldn't be smart.'

'Not smart, I see. I tell you what would be smart, catch the damn killer.'

'He'll be caught, sir, he'll be caught.'

20

Whenever he returned to Romania, Sir Nicu was amused to see the face of the passport control fellow when they checked his documents. His name was Ceaușescu Niculae, no relation to the dead one, but his mother (a well-known fortune teller in their home county of Teleorman) had foreseen that Party Secretary Dej would die in 1965 and that Ceaușescu would replace him. Of course, back in 1963, when her first son was born, no one knew exactly who Ceaușescu was, but she named him Ceaușescu anyway, and their surname was Niculae, so a star was born.

His fellow Romas called him Sir Nicu, both before and after the fall of Communism, because he was a calm, settled kind of guy, who would only countenance violence in the most extreme of cases, but nevertheless seemed to effortlessly lord it over everyone else. He could win everyone over with his words, he wasn't greedy, he was generous, so everyone was happy. He was not quite as wealthy as he might have been, but he was content and well-regarded. Immediately after the revolution, he got involved in all sorts of dodgy affairs and had money to burn. But he soon realised this wasn't the path he wanted to be on long-term, so he moved onto legal businesses. The only link to his old way of life was his team of debt-collectors, whom he still sent in sporadically to help out friends or when things got really out of hand. It was the head of his debt-collecting team, Bean, who'd been found in the Andronache forest, so Sir Nicu returned hurriedly from his business trip to Lebanon.

Otopeni Airport was full of security guards and diplomatic corps, prepped for the arrival of the French President. He finally got through passport control, picked up his luggage and left the airport flanked by his two bodyguards.

Back at HQ, it was quiet. There were very few who knew of his links to Bean and his gang. He went to the top floor of the office building, where two members of his executive team were waiting for him together with two senior detectives. He offered them all presents from Lebanon – gold jewellery for their wives, perfume for their mistresses, cigars and cognac for themselves. Then he dived right in.

'You're sure it was Sword who killed Bean?'

'Very likely. The blow is almost identical to the previous one, but the cut is smaller. So it's possible that the killer was using a different weapon. Plus, there's a blow to the back of the head. In all of the previous cases, Sword struck just once, straight in the neck.' Commander Movilă of the Bucharest Police laid out the photos of all the victims. 'In this case, he was struck from behind, probably fainted, and then was killed.'

'So, what are the implications?'

'It could mean that it's not Sword. It could be someone squaring things off with Bean or with yourself. And they used the MO of the serial killer to escape detection.'

'I see. But who is Sword?'

Movilă had to smile.

'That's the big, disgraceful mystery for us in the police. We have no idea. Neither does Interpol, nor even the FBI. If you want my opinion, I don't think he murdered Bean. Look at your guy's recent enemies, see who hates you and who is powerful enough to order such a hit.'

'According to the papers, Sword could well be a special police unit doing the dirty work.'

'That would be a neat solution. But that's for American TV series, not for the Romanian police.'

'So why are you incapable of catching him, if he's not one of yours?'

'Because he's too good to allow himself to get caught. He must have some police or army experience. He knows all the rules. Even after ten crimes or so, there has never been an eyewitness.'

Sir Nicu looked down at the photos, without really seeing them. Bean and he went back fifteen or more years. He was the brains, Bean was the brawn of the operation. Losing one of the most notorious fist-fighters in Bucharest was going to have an impact on his business. Even more so, if the killer proved to be someone other than Sword.

'I always meant to ask – not sure if this is the right moment – but why was his nickname Bean?'

'Because he'd beat people up so thoroughly they became like bean paste in his hands. He was one of the toughest guys I've ever known, so I find it hard to believe that a single man with a sword could take him down like that. Besides, what on earth would he be doing in the forest? I think he was killed elsewhere and then moved. Which again points to a different killer from Sword.'

'Maybe he went to the woods for a little nookie?'

'Not him! He had a house for his wife and kids, another house for his mistress, and a flat where he could take all his one-night stands. No need to go somewhere so uncomfortable for sex. No, I tell you, he was murdered elsewhere and then taken to the forest.'

Sir Nicu thought for a while, then he said: 'Tell you what, Commander. I'm pretty sure that my Bean was killed by another gang, but I really want you to catch this Sword guy. I've never made a big deal about being a gypsy, and I hate all this talk about bad feelings between gypsies and Romanians. But I can't have a madman going around targeting gypsies. Please tell everyone that I am offering a reward of a hundred thousand euros for any information leading to the capture of this criminal.'

'Are you sure that's not excessive? Rusu's TV station offered a hundred thousand lei.'

'You heard right – a hundred thousand euros. And if there's more than one person who's got useful information, I'm prepared to give more.'

After the policemen left, carrying their presents carefully, Sir Nicu turned to his senior execs.

'I want you to publicise the offer of a reward via all possible channels, papers, TV, radio, adverts.'

'Do you think that will help?'

'It'll certainly make people think that Bean was murdered by Sword, not by a rival gang.'

21

The Prime Minister found out about Sword's ninth victim over the phone, from one of his special advisers. It was a rainy Sunday in October and he was at the official holiday residence in Scroviştea, a place he absolutely loathed. The ceilings were low, it was as dark as a grave, the furniture was outdated and it was buzzing with special forces teams. The only halfway pleasant thing was the terrace overlooking the lake – but the lake itself was filthy and it stank. There was an air of rot and decay about the whole place. But the President, whose villa was next door to this one, had insisted that they should have dinner together.

Dinner should have started half an hour ago, but no doubt there would be further delays because of the news. In the hallway, he could hear his wife's high-pitched tone of displeasure, arguing with one of the guards. He was holed up in his study, as far away from the entrance as possible, playing chess on the computer. His predecessor used to play draughts with his bodyguards or head of staff. At least chess was more civilised, more strategic.

The phone rang again. It was one of the President's men, warning him that there would be further delays and whispering in a conspiratorial fashion: 'They found another body, you know.'

The PM didn't have the heart to tell him that he already knew. The presidential adviser recited all the facts he knew. The victim was a gypsy, a criminal, and had been found by some children behind the bins on the Moşilor Boulevard. A single blow to the throat. He was a car thief and was killed outside one of the bodyshops where he chopped up cars for spare parts. His name was Adrian Hogea, known as Klaxon.

After the presidential advisor hung up, the PM switched off the remaining lamp and stood for a while in the dark, deep in thought. Then he picked up the second phone, the black one that his bodyguards called the 'superconnected one'. He asked to be connected to the Head of Foreign Intelligence. Less than a minute later, he had Calin on the line.

'Hello, how are you?'

'Prime Minister … honestly? I was asleep.'

'So you haven't heard the news yet.'

'Someone called a minute or two before you did. Where are you?'

'At Scoroviştea.'

'Oh, has the President called for a special meeting?'

'No, I was invited for dinner before we heard the news. I just wanted to tell you that I read the reports you sent me yesterday and I'm deeply worried. I've also spoken to a friend of mine, Ben Stark, who's a British banker and he's also concerned about these Roma murders. I've known Ben for more than twenty years now and he's not normally the kind of man to make a fuss about any ethnic minorities. That's why his questions about this affair make me think that we've got a giant of a problem on our hands.'

'Yes, sir. Our research shows a growing concern regarding this issue in the West. There's been some meddling from within the country as well – sending transcripts of TV and radio programmes, that kind of thing. I suspect that Iliescu and his foundation are behind all of that. He's been spreading the rumour that the police are conspiring with the murderer. This damn rumour has caught on, it's nearly impossible to budge.'

'What are the chances of the killer getting arrested?'

'The latest police report clearly states that they are clueless. They do know that the latest crime before this one did not have Sword's MO.'

'I know that. But the first crime was nearly three months ago. How can they be clueless still? Could it be that the rumours are true, that the police are in cahoots with the murderer?'

'Certainly not! We've infiltrated the police thoroughly – as have the special services, the Internal Intelligence and so on. On top of that, most of their senior officers are corrupt, so the criminal gangs would have been the first to find out about any developments. I heard that two of the top police officers were called to the offices of a gang leader yesterday, and that he offered a reward of a hundred thousand euros to catch Sword. It's all so meticulously planned that my fear is that it's some external intelligence agency messing with us.'

'So what are you going to do about it?'
'We're analysing the information.'
'Anything else? More actionable?'
'You know we've suggested that the Minister of the Interior be replaced.'
'Why? Do you think he's to blame for anything?'
'Of course not. But we have to find a scapegoat and a new minister would have a short period of grace. During that time, they might even catch the killer. I don't know if you caught that talk show yesterday?'
'I heard about it...'
'Well, he showed me the messages they received from viewers during and right after the show. They had eight times as many calls as usual and three-quarters of them were extremely hostile towards the Roma. Violent, hateful remarks, suggesting lynching, executions, hanging, all sorts. It's not the Roma I'm scared of, but the Romanians.'

The PM's assistant entered the room and signalled that he had a message from the President.

'Listen, Calin, I need to go now. Thank you for your update.'
'You're welcome.'

Unfortunately, the message was merely that dinner had been delayed yet again, and that two cabinet ministers would be joining them. The Prime Minister sighed and asked his assistant to bring him a little toast and yoghurt. He then settled back in front of his computer and at least had the satisfaction of beating the chess app.

22

The President's office was full of people, laying out cables, testing microphones, setting up lights, rearranging the flags behind the desk, moving the furniture. The President was about to give a live interview on national TV. The interviewer was Leo Trandafir, who was currently checking his notes while a make-up artist dabbed his face with a powder puff.

The President checked that everything was going as planned, then retired to the smaller office behind the main one, together with his security adviser and the acupuncturist, who stuck a few needles in the palm of his hands and behind his ear, in an attempt to soothe his back pain.

'So you've talked with Leo? There'll be no nasty surprises?'

'Not at all. He's a very good boy, very keen. Next spring, you'll propose him for a directorial position with the National Audiovisual Council. He wanted to know if you were going to address the Sword issue at all.'

'We are here to discuss the visit of the French President, nothing else.'

'Yes, but you can't just ignore a burning domestic issue.'

'The French President's visit is a domestic issue as well, as are all my diplomatic efforts. It will lead to European integration, foreign investment in our country, economic reform. That's what we should be talking about, not about why we are incapable of catching a serial killer. I'm not going to make a fool of myself. There's nothing to say about that.'

'You should announce draconian measures.'

'You don't announce such measures, you simply introduce them! And stop telling me to change the Minister of the Interior. I don't like him much either, but I can't turn the whole party against me. The PM doesn't want to replace him. Now that's a clever man, the PM. The only thing he talks about is the economy, which no one understands, and the only thing he does is play chess on his computer. Does anyone ever ask the Prime Minister about Sword? No. And he is the actual executive arm of the government, he's the one who appointed the Minister of the Interior. No, it's me the press is hounding. I refuse to talk about this matter.'

The special adviser on communications and media image rushed into the room. 'I've brought you a few quotes – Lincoln, Kogălniceanu and a few Frenchmen, including Malraux. I've got the originals in French, in case you want to read them.'

The President glanced at the papers and sat down again. His back was still quite painful.

'I've got a rather unpleasant piece of news as well,' his media adviser continued.

SWORD

'OK, let's hear it. Who's insulting me now?'

'No, it's just that Rusu has announced a film premiere at the same time on his TV channel, which could steal quite a few of our viewers.'

'What do you mean, he's announced it? When did that happen?'

'Well, the regular TV programme was showing an older film, but he changed it suddenly this morning and now it's a very recent cinema release, so a lot of people will want to watch it.'

'This morning... and you're only telling me now?'

'Sir, you know that we have no TVs here to follow matters. In fact, I just found out about it by accident, from my wife.'

'What do you mean? You have no TVs?'

'Well, they are all broken, but not broken enough to be replaced. We are waiting for them to be repaired.'

The President looked imploringly at his security adviser.

'Mr President, do you want me to resolve that? Shall I call Rusu?'

'How long have we got?'

'Forty-five minutes until the interview. I could phone him and ask him to delay the start of the film or change it to something less interesting.'

The security adviser left the room in a hurry. The President sighed and slid down to a prone position on the sofa.

'What do you suggest, Marinescu?' he asked his media adviser. 'Should I mention Sword or not?'

'Heaven forbid, no!'

'But won't the journalists rant at me tomorrow?'

'Let them! They'll do that anyway, because you have nothing further to tell them about the case. Besides, the papers aren't that important. Only ten per cent of Romanians read the papers. Eighty per cent of them watch TV news. So better stick to what's important.'

'You're right. The only thing I'm afraid of is that they'll say I'm boasting about my international successes while the country is burning.'

'They probably will. But it's still better than appearing tongue-tied on national TV. After all, you don't have anything new to say about Sword, do you?'

'Actually, I have lots to say on this subject. I could say that gypsies really are a problem in our country today, a far greater problem than the Russians or the Hungarians. And that we are caught in a double bind. If we try to invest money in gypsy communities, there would be loud protest from precisely those do-gooders who are now clamouring for the killer's head. And if we introduce tougher punishments and custodial sentences, then the EU will protest. Sword is merely the start of something that could drag on and on. The US has had this problem with their black people for decades. What's worse, if the economy contracts, it will get even more hostile. I could tell them how powerful these gypsy criminal gangs are and how corrupt our police and justice system are. Do you know that one of our major party donors is part of a smuggling operation involving two gypsy gangs? And that the opposition party is partly funded by a gang trafficking weapons and drugs, working hand-in-hand with a terrorist group from the Middle East?

'But no, I can't say any of that. Because I'm all alone here, surrounded by people who don't even have working TVs in their offices. But let me tell you this: if we lose the next election – which looks likely at this moment in time – then it will be downhill all the way. Romania will become a paradise for criminals.'

The security adviser returned with a smile on his face.

'Rusu agreed to delay the start of the film.'

The President stood up carefully, gathered his papers and straightened his tie for the interview.

23

The next morning, presidential media adviser Marinescu was reading the press monitor and examining closely all the papers attacking the President. In the live interview on national TV, the President hadn't mentioned Sword at all – in fact, he hadn't even been asked about it. Naturally, that meant that Ionescu and Cârstea had written tough editorials lamenting the fact. The tabloids sponsored by the newspaper tycoon Vasilescu were also very critical, but that was to be expected. He seemed to have established close links to Radu Rădulescu. However, what he did not expect was the aggressive tone of Cornel Ardeleanu's editorial.

When I was a child, I would spend every day during the summer holidays taking the goats out to graze. Even at the weekend.

Sundays were always a bit special. My father was a good friend of the local priest. They'd been through the war together. Every Sunday evening, the priest (who was a widower) would come to dine with us. My mother would cook wonderful stuff that we'd usually expect to see at Christmas or Easter. And the priest would tell stories. He was a well-educated, well-travelled man. My first glimpse of the world of culture came from this man, Father Cernea, because neither my father nor mother – hardworking, honest folk though they were – nor the school could give me that. That's why, when I went out with the goats on a Sunday, I would tell myself that in the evening I would get good food and interesting anecdotes from Father Cernea, and the day would just fly by…

But then one day, I must have been in Year Eight by then, I got caught in a thunderstorm while I was out with the goats and was soaked through to the skin. I got home, washed and changed quickly to be ready for the visit. When I got to the dinner table, my father told me that the priest would not be with us that night. He'd gone to Alba on urgent business. But a little while later, I heard my father telling my mother that Father Cernea was blind drunk and sleeping it off. I'd seen drunk people before, but I could not hide my disappointment. I'd been waiting for our meeting all day and he let me down simply because he was drunk.

That's the way I felt last night when I watched the President's TV interview. Who on earth are his advisers, because they couldn't have given him worse advice? The President's audience last night was predominantly working class. Intellectuals and urban elites were watching other channels, films and stupid game shows. But the ordinary working people – farmers, industrial workers – were watching him. Hoping that he would tell them something they could understand. But no. He spoke about France and the USA, about the EU and Germany, about harmonisation and reform. He spouted lots of numbers that no-one could relate to, and ended with a quote in French.

Nothing about poverty, nothing about hunger, nothing about the minuscule pensions, nothing about the hospitals in which people die before their time, nothing about unemployment and this hard life that we all live. As a president, he should care about all of that. What's even worse, not a single word about this Sword case that has been plaguing our nation for the past three months. The country is divided, there have been some serious interethnic hostilities and yet the President can find nothing to say about this.

Of course I am aware how important international relations are, and I don't want to deny the President's contribution in raising our country's profile after the dreadful period of isolation it suffered previously. But I honestly think the President is drunk. Drunk on power and flattery. So drunk that he doesn't realise that there are millions of people hanging on his every word, waiting for a sign that he is awake and aware of what is happening in his parish. After last night's interview, I can safely say that the President is no longer with us. He has sat himself at the table with sycophants and believes that those yes-men actually represent the Romanian people.

Marinescu called Calin and finally got through, after several transfers:

'What's up with Cornel? Has he gone crazy?'

'I tried to call him this morning, but he wasn't up yet. What does the President say?'

'I haven't spoken to him yet, but it's going to be a shitstorm. Cornel was one of ours. After all we've done for him. Two years ago he was a nobody. Now he's got money and influence, and we're the ones who helped him get both, as you well know.'

'You know he's a bit of a maverick.'

'This has nothing to do with being a maverick. This looks to me like bribery. From what I've heard, Cornel won't work for less than ten thousand. That's for articles on economic matters, for politics the fee is higher still. I heard personally from a party leader that he paid Cornel thirty thousand for an article NOT to appear just before the party conference.'

'I've heard about that – the sum is exaggerated, though. But this time I don't think it's about the money. After all, he criticises Rădulescu as well.'

'It's not just Rădulescu who can bribe people in this country, you know.'

Marinescu's PA came into the room and mouthed that the President was waiting to see him.

'My boss is calling me. I'd better go and commit hara-kiri.'

'Why?'

'I was the one who advised him not to mention Sword.'

'And he disagreed with you?'

'Not at all, but that's not the point... Anyway, please talk to Cornel and tell him to stop.'

'You can bet on it. But he is a bit of a weirdo.'

'He wasn't such a weirdo when he was asking for our help to get the Austrians to buy out his rag of a paper, with all the debts and the court cases against him. I had to use all my persuasive skills and phone around, calling in favours. The President himself had to intervene with the Austrians. Cornel is a piece of shit – and I've heard lots of juicy gossip about him from his ex-wife. He's not to be trusted. And now I'd better go.'

24

Nenișor Vasile's villa on Lake Mogoșoaia had often been the backdrop for political meetings about the future of the country, meetings which usually ended with barbecues and fine wine from his cellar. At four in the morning his wife would then prepare a tripe soup for them all as a hangover cure. If it was a fasting day, he refused to serve them any meat, but would offer delicious vegetarian options – stuffed vine leaves and aubergines, cheese, beans, vegetarian stew and of course his fine wine. If you were really weak, he might even let you get away with a bit of fish, because it didn't count as meat. Vasile was quite conservative in his own way. You had to fast with him. And you could only visit with your official wife, no mistresses allowed.

Radu Rădulescu was currently sitting on Nenișor's covered terrace, wrapped up in a warm blanket, sipping his mulled wine. It was cold, but the sky was clear. You could see the stars reflected in the still waters of the lake. There was a hint of winter in the air, amidst the smell of burnt leaves. Rădulescu was the only guest.

A Brahms violin concerto could be heard from the living room. They'd been discussing politics for nearly three hours now: opinion polls, what was going well, how the current President's popularity was on the wane. He was currently being attacked by his own party. Meanwhile, opportunists were rejoining the opposition party.

That's the sure sign of victory, they agreed. When the rats leave the sinking ship and board the rival ship. Three years previously, when Rădulescu's defeat seemed imminent, there were daily defections. People stopped answering the phone. Journalists who had been given high visibility thanks to Rădulescu were going across to the other side. Just look at them now, returning to the fold, their tails between their legs! So were the businessmen. Three years ago they'd stopped funding the election campaign, despite the fact that many of their businesses had got off the ground or had their debts forgiven thanks to Rădulescu's party. Now they were paying for forgiveness.

Nenişor had been one of the few people who had not forgotten his friend after the election defeat. He called him the very next day and invited him to this villa. His wife cooked an unforgettable fried chicken with garlic sauce and polenta, followed by Moldovan doughballs. Nenişor had played the violin for him. Rădulescu had battled on… and now, in a year's time, he would be back in power. And he would get his revenge on all those who'd betrayed him. He had jotted down people on his mental blacklist. He knew exactly what he was going to tell them, and how he was going to punish each one of them.

He even felt somewhat sorry for the poor President. His security adviser had been on the phone a short while ago, begging him to ask for the resignation of the Minister of the Interior, because he'd lost the support of his own party. The world was crumbling beneath them and they'd started sticking daggers into each other.

'If this assassin kills just a few more, we'll be in power even before the elections.'

'Yes, if they don't catch him,' said Nenişor.

'They won't. I've spoken to all the senior police officers, and they haven't got a single useful lead.'

'I keep wondering who this guy is. Do you think he could be one of your party members? After all, you've been going up in the polls since the murders started.'

'Please don't joke about these things. I am genuinely surprised that the President hasn't accused us yet of being behind these crimes, to destabilise the country and his reforms.'

'Of course, it would be a feather in his cap if they did catch him.'

'*If* they catch him. But I think we'll see the back of Mr President long before that happens. We did a good job with Cornel Ardeleanu, now we need to find someone external to deliver another slap to his face. Perhaps someone from the US. Where it hurts the most. But fine, Nenişor, my party will back you this time if you ask again for the resignation of the Minister of the Interior.'

'And who are they going to put in his place?'

'It doesn't matter. If things continue like this, I can ask for a snap election in three months. The truth is, I wouldn't like to be in the President's place right now. All the press is against him, even his own sycophants. Ardeleanu only cost us twenty thousand dollars. And he'll continue delivering, talking about interethnic conflict.'

'There hasn't really been any of that...'

'No, but people abroad don't have a clue about the real facts. And it's the people abroad that the President cares about. He's in a real bind. If he catches the killer, he has to punish him. But the fact that Sword is doing away with criminals makes him quite popular with a certain part of the electorate who vote for him. So, if he punishes Sword too severely, he will lose votes. If he doesn't punish him enough, then the West will condemn him. Never mind the fact that we could get a hostile environment very soon.'

'You're not going to try and sell me that old myth that the gypsies are going to revolt.'

'Not the gypsies. The Romanians. I've had some indications from the intelligence community that tensions are growing in certain parts of the country. All it needs is one small spark and the tinderbox will explode. You simply cannot imagine what that could lead to... Now give me another glass of that mulled wine, I'm starting to get cold here.'

25

Cyprus at the end of November was absolutely delightful. It was probably delightful all year round, but at this time of year there were fewer tourists, less noise and chaos. Admittedly, Paphos was still full of British pensioners, escaping the fog and rain back home. The restaurants served fish and chips and full English breakfast with sausages, baked beans and crispy bacon. Everyone spoke English and even the cars were on the wrong side of the road, like in Britain.

In the part of town beyond the castle you could find some of the most beautiful Ancient Greek mosaics, remarkably well-preserved, but also jewellery shops and bars full of escorts from Eastern Europe. Amidst all of these, you might also stumble across a steel and glass monstrosity, a conference centre where the international conference about the rights of ethnic minorities was taking place.

The first two days at the conference had been quite enjoyable, almost like a holiday, but now Dobre, Under-Secretary at the Romanian Ministry of Foreign Affairs, was starting to sweat. They'd been discussing Romania for over an hour. A former US congressman, now president of a foundation for the preservation of ethnic minorities, had launched a vicious attack against the alleged discrimination against ethnic minorities in Romania. Two Hungarians from international NGOs and a German Green Party member chimed in. A Swedish woman referred to the terrible discrimination against HIV-positive children in Romania, and then a Dutch MP stood up to protest against the persecution of Protestant sects. Dobre felt he had to intervene, even though the auditorium was half-empty. Those who had presented during the first two days had probably already left the conference to go shopping or enjoy a short boat trip on the Mediterranean.

'I'd like to point out a few things, 'Dobre began. 'I consider any discussion about the integrity of the national borders to be a highly dangerous one. Transylvania is part of Romania – there is nothing further to discuss there. As far as I know, Hungary has signed all the international treaties regarding border arrangements. What I would like to say is that I feel that the discussion of minorities at this conference has been disappointingly superficial. And I simply cannot understand how anybody could treat this lightly, after Kosovo and the whole tragedy in Yugoslavia. In that explosive situation in the Balkans, you have to admit that Romania has been a pillar of stability. Why try to create problems where there aren't any? We've got plenty of real problems: economic, social, political. But we don't have interethnic conflict. If you want proof of that, the party of the Hungarian minority is part of the coalition government. How can you talk about discrimination in this case?'

The chair of the panel nodded and was about to move on to the next topic, but the American Patrick Johnson lifted his hand. The chair warned him that he could only let the discussion go on for another fifteen minutes.

'Mr Under-Secretary, what have you got to tell us about the serial murders of members of the Roma community over the past few months? Are you telling us we're exaggerating in that matter as well?'

'What can I say? The newly capitalist Romanian society is not without its problems. Criminality is one of these problems. On the whole, there is far less violence in Romania than in many other countries. The case that Mr Johnson is referring to is probably one of the first known instances of a serial killer in our country. The murderer seems to select his victims not necessarily because they are spokespeople for their minority, but according to criminal records. I don't think this has anything to do with racial hatred.'

'Can you tell us anything more about the Roma and how they are responding to this?'

'I'm not a specialist in matters pertaining to the Roma population. All I can tell you is that they represent more of a social problem rather than an ethnic one. The last census recorded seven hundred thousand Romas, but we believe the actual figure is closer to two million, since a majority of the Roma population prefer to identify themselves as Romanian. They have a higher birth rate than ethnic Romanians, so that number is growing.'

'Does that pose a problem for you? What would happen if the number is significantly reduced?' With that zinger, Patrick Johnson put down his microphone.

'I don't understand what you are asking me. We cannot change birth rates. It is quite likely that within the next thirty years, the percentage of Romas as part of the total population of Romania will rise to fifteen or twenty per cent. You are surely not suggesting that we would want to organise a little genocide to solve that problem? Or that we are working together with the serial killer to scare a minority group? We cannot accept your insinuation, not even as a joke. The murderer is obviously a madman, someone who has been brainwashed by far too many brutal American films and thinks this is how he will get his fifteen minutes of fame.'

26

The TV voiceover man managed to make himself heard over the applause of the audience and the sounds of the orchestra as he boomed out: 'Ladies and gentlemen, please welcome your host of 'Romanian Wrap-Up', Alin Dobrescu…'

The applause intensified, the music got louder and their host appeared, full of smiles as usual. He cracked his usual jokes about the month of December, Christmas presents, how the snow would inevitably catch all of the mayors by surprise. Then he continued: 'Ladies and gentlemen, my guest this evening is the Minister of the Interior.'

There was sporadic clapping as the Minister walked into the studio and sat down opposite Dobrescu on the yellow sofa.

'How are you, sir? How is it going with Operation Clean Streets?'

'I'm fine and the operation is going well.'

'How many have you arrested so far?'

'To date, we've detained around a thousand people. Not all of them were taken into custody, but we've managed to eliminate a few human trafficking and drug-trafficking networks. And we're not done yet.'

'You know what I don't understand? Why don't you legalise prostitution? Let the ladies ply their trade, keep everyone happy and save precious resources for more serious crimes.'

'My job is to apply the law, not to change it.'

'Why not change it? You're in the Cabinet. Still. I heard that you beat the PM at chess, so you might be out at the next cabinet reshuffle.'

'Nonsense. I've never played chess with the Prime Minister. Besides, if there is a cabinet reshuffle, these decisions are made elsewhere, and the Prime Minister is likely to listen to them to keep the party happy.'

'When you say elsewhere, you mean the President?'

'I'm not here to discuss such matters. A minister can be changed by the PM or the President, or following a vote in Parliament, or if the party decides they no longer can support him. If I get 'reshuffled', it will be through one of those mechanisms.'

'Personally, sir, I think you are one of the better government ministers. I've never hidden the fact that I don't think much of the current government. The policies and measures you've taken at your own Ministry have often been the only concrete and effective thing happening here. That's why I hope that all these rumours about a reshuffle are untrue – because it would be a pity for the country to lose one of its best ministers for the sake of political games.'

'Thank you, I fear your words are giving yet more ammunition to those who want to get rid of me. But let's talk about the real reason why I'm here. Sword.'

'Yes. Sword. Why have you failed to catch him?'

'Do you want me to be blunt?'

'Yes, please.'

'You see, just like societies evolve, so do criminals. If society progresses faster than the criminals, then we stand a chance of catching them. If, however, it's the other way round... I'm not here to defend my position. I'm here to defend a profession. The police are unjustly reviled in this country. They get blamed for everything. It might be true that a few of them still have old-fashioned ideas, but on the whole they've moved on, but public perception of them hasn't. For all their faults, the police are the only effective barrier between the public and the criminals. I'm not denying that some of them have been proven to be corrupt, but most of them are honest and passionate about justice. And they are not richly rewarded for their work. They face danger on a daily basis, yet they have low salaries and no special perks. In Ceaușescu's era criminals used to steal maize from the state farm or destroy public property. Nowadays, they've got better weapons and faster cars than the police, and they are not afraid of deploying both. Right now, criminals are slowly but surely gaining the upper hand over the police.'

'I was asking you specifically about Sword.'

'I know... and the usual answer in such cases is that we cannot discuss a matter which is currently under investigation. However, I want to be very clear about the distinction between the police case Sword and the political issue Sword. These serial killings with a punitive and ethnic component to them have given ammunition to all sorts of political arguments by the main opposition party. I believe that both Nenişor Vasile and Radu Rădulescu are playing a dangerous game of fuelling and exacerbating ethnic tensions between Romanians and Romas, with the sole purpose of discrediting the current government both within the borders of our country and beyond. I've spoken to several leaders of the Roma community who are shocked by Nenişor's interventions. If politicians hadn't got involved in all of this, the Sword case would have been a simple police matter and we would have resolved it sooner or later. It has now become so much more than that! They are using each new victim as an excuse to make political statements. And it's not just the politicians who are using these murders for their own nefarious purposes. Let me tell you – although I am sure that I will be criticised for giving out confidential information – that one of the victims was almost certainly not killed by Sword, but by a copycat killer.'

'I've heard those rumours, yes. And it's not surprising, since rumours are all we've got to go on. The other persistent rumour is that the killer is part of a special police force.'

'Yes, I've heard the idiotic conspiracy theory that there is such a thing as a special "brigade of death", a secret arm of the police, who assassinates undesirable people. Let me reassure your viewers and every single citizen of this country that the police are not at all involved in these murders, and that there are no such brigades in Romania.'

'Sadly, one might indeed say that the police are completely uninvolved... Anyway, Minister, I hope you catch your killer soon, regardless of how some of us might feel about the justification for his actions. And I also hope you survive the political storm.'

27

It had been raining non-stop for three days in Bucharest, turning into sleet and snow by evening. By the following morning, the snow melted but the pavements remained dirty and slippery, and pedestrians risked getting splashed with mud from the passing cars. A further icy gust of wind and rain forced Sanda to find shelter in the multi-storey department store right next to the bus stop. If the bus came now, it would be completely packed, she told herself. Besides, she had just received an end-of-project bonus, so she was inclined to do a bit of shopping therapy. Since her divorce ten years ago, Sanda had learnt to live alone and enjoy life to the full. There were no major accomplishments to celebrate, but after fifty years of living under Communism and then during the painful transition, she made the most of every little bit of good news she could find.

As a child she had been part of a national youth sports squad. She had never been the best, though, so she learnt to be happy with what she had. National sports back then meant a little extra food, training camps at the seaside (her parents would never have had the money to send her there) and a few competitions in neighbouring socialist countries. There was no need to feel guilty about spending a bit of money on herself occasionally – she had a flat, she didn't need a car, and she had no-one for whom to save up the money.

She always stopped and stared at the electrical gadgets and white goods, but could never quite commit to buying anything. The shop was busy and a few people bumped into her as she stood there. She was bending down to examine a smoothie maker more closely, when she saw the sales assistant throwing her an anxious look, as if she was trying to warn her of something. She turned round and caught a young boy with his hand in her bag. She shouted at him and slapped him. The boy swore and tried to pull the bag off her shoulder. Another boy ran up and threatened her with a sharpened screwdriver.

'Drop the bag now!'

A third, slightly older youth, showed up and told the other two to give up and run. Sanda had grabbed the younger lad by the collar and was not letting go, although he was kicking as if he were possessed. His two accomplices ran off. By this point, the onlookers had realised what was going on and had surrounded Sanda and the pickpocket. Sanda was still yelling and clinging onto the thief. The boy suddenly went down on his haunches and then sprang back up again, hitting Sanda squarely on the chin with his head. Sanda fell over and the boy escaped, pulling out a knife and slightly injuring one of the men who tried to stop him.

As he reached the staircase, two security guards raced towards him. The boy managed to dodge the first, while the second man failed to grab him, so shoved him instead. The boy lost his balance and, at the speed he was going, he flew right over the railings and fell all the way down to the ground floor. People started screaming. The two guards rushed down the stairs, but it was too late. A pool of blood was slowly seeping through from underneath the body.

28

The Prime Minister had been trying, unsuccessfully, to get a word in edgeways in the heated argument between two of his cabinet members, both leaders of smaller parties in his coalition. He had been forced to listen to all sorts of compromising personal details about both of them, and, worst of all, after washing all of their dirty linen in public, they'd turned to him in the expectation that he would somehow resolve their conflict. He refused to get involved in their dispute, although he knew that they would probably carry it further, in parliament, in the papers and on national TV.

In less than an hour, he was due to hold negotiations with the representatives from the World Bank. Once he'd got rid of his two ministers, he decided to play another game of chess. He always chose black. His motto since childhood had been to let the others make the first move. The phone rang. He picked it up reluctantly – it was the President.

'We've got a problem. Let me read it out loud. *"The bloody ritual of interethnic conflict in the Balkans shows no signs of diminishing. For ten years, Europe witnessed the terrible war in former Yugoslavia, involving three religions and six distinct nations, with the spectres of nationalism and ethnic cleansing reappearing from the ashes of Fascism and Communism, and condemning tens of thousands of people to death. An uneasy truce has descended upon the region, but the Macedonians and Albanians are still at each other's throats, the Serbs and the Croats are by no means reconciled, and the Turkish minority in Bulgaria continues to be oppressed. What we are witnessing now is a shift to the north. Romania is no stranger to xenophobic and anti-semitic tendencies, but this week things seem to have escalated and the country is on the brink of a civil war. Of course, the persecution of minorities is nothing new: we have heard plenty about the plight of the Hungarians, we have seen the Jewish community decimated during the war and being forced to emigrate during Ceausescu's era. The German population has also largely abandoned the country and moved abroad. Now it's the turn of the Roma community. Estimated at between seven hundred thousand and two million, the Roma population is marginalised and living in extreme poverty. The VP of the Romanian Foundation for the Rights of Ethnic Minorities, Andrei Gabriel Iliescu, states that if you are a member of an ethnic minority, you are doomed to fail in Romania today. There are no politicians to fight their corner – with the exception of the Hungarian Democratic Union MPs. Two days ago a fourteen-year-old boy was brutally attacked by police in a hypermarket in the centre of Bucharest. The boy in question, Ionel Buzatu, was an ethnic Roma, the fourth child in a family of eight, living in a slum on the edge of Bucharest. His parents couldn't afford to send him to school. He was working on the black market. Romanian labour legislation seems reluctant to deal with the exploitation of minors. The police tried to claim that little Ionel was a pickpocket, but his father Vasile, 55, says his son had never stolen a thing in his life. Ionel is merely the latest in a long list of fatalities. For the past four months, Romas are being systematically executed throughout Bucharest by a serial killer known only as Sword. Our police sources confirm that there are so-called death squads sanctioned by the government and operating throughout the capital, and that they are probably the ones behind these crimes."*

'Who wrote this crap? It's childish and very easy to prove wrong.'

'Jean-Christophe Boullier, the France Presse correspondent in Bucharest. And this document has been making the rounds among all the other foreign press agencies. You and I have ostensibly been ordering our death squads to kill innocent Roma activists such as Fly and Slut and Butcher. And let's not forget Klaxon, who was sent packing from Germany a few years ago. Back then he was branded a criminal by the West, now he is an ethnic hero. I have to admit I never expected to be confronted by such flies and sluts when I entered politics. I've invited the French ambassador to come and explain how this is possible. I'm asking you to join me at this meeting.'

'But you know I'm not good with such things.'

'You are the head of the Romanian government, which now stands accused of sending death squads to deal with its undesirable citizens. I would like you to call for an emergency cabinet meeting. I myself will convene our Security Council, and we really need to take an official position on this. We need to organise press conferences, demand that France Presse apologises and pays us compensation. We have to call all the other European ambassadors, with their foreign ministers. Lots to do. We cannot allow them to put us in the same pot as Yugoslavia and claim that we are on the brink of civil war. All the political parties have to protest, we have to present a united front. Can you imagine what a disastrous effect it would have on our image abroad? On our foreign investors?'

'No worse than our corruption and dodgy legislation. Serious investors don't get scared off by newspaper reports. They do their homework.'

'Still, by ten o'clock tomorrow morning I want to have your proposal on actionable next steps on my desk. You should have received all the details by now from the intelligence agencies.'

'I have indeed, but I haven't had the time to look at them.'

'Well, please make sure that you do. And now, good luck with the World Bank!'

The Prime Minister opened the thick envelope from the intelligence agencies. He sighed at the volume of the paperwork, then asked for a pot of fruit tea and phoned the Minister of Foreign Affairs.

29

The President was casually dressed in a tracksuit as he came downstairs after a brief afternoon nap. He had even had time to look at his precious stamp collection and admire a rare Venetian specimen. That's why he was in a good mood. The same couldn't be said of the people waiting for him in the dining room: Stoicescu, head of the Intelligence Services, Calin, head of Foreign Intelligence, and his media adviser Marinescu. The security adviser joined them shortly afterwards.

'I've managed to convince the French ambassador to replace the France Presse correspondent in Bucharest. However, the Prime Minister was about as useful as a ton of bricks. As per usual. He called the Minister of Foreign Affairs, growled at him a little, and that was it. The Minister of Foreign Affairs called his under-secretaries, growled at them a little, and that was him done. One of the under-secretaries called Marinescu and said that they considered it to be a problem with Romania's image abroad and that this fell into his remit. So, mission accomplished – as always, by me alone. Funny how the whole diplomatic corps never seems able to help in moments of crisis. No one has contacted any of the foreign embassies … because they are supposedly too busy with the organisation of the upcoming OSCE Summit in Bucharest. And I'm willing to bet that, with all of their careful preparations, they will still have problems with the sound system, or there will be a power cut, or someone will refuse to let some foreign VIP into the conference hall.'

'I guess you've heard about Rădulescu's statement in front of the Senate,' the security adviser said, barging into the conversation. 'We should have demanded the resignation of the Minister of the Interior ourselves. Now we have to do it at Rădulescu's initiative.'

'Well, then we refuse to do it,' Stoicescu said calmly.

'But the new minister has already picked his team.'

'No problem, he just needs to be patient a little longer.'

'If he doesn't get fired, Rădulescu will ask him for proof … and it will look bad for us once again,' protested Calin.

'How do you know he doesn't have proof?' Stoicescu was almost ethereal and serene.

'Stop fooling around. We should have got rid of him a long time ago. We've shot ourselves in the foot now and are giving brownie points to the opposition,' the security adviser was tapping his foot nervously as he sat down in the armchair furthest away from Stoicescu.

The President had perked up.

'Sandu, do you think he has got proof that Rădulescu and Nenişor have been instigating interethnic conflict?'

'I do indeed. But if you don't mind, sir, I would prefer to discuss such matters with you alone, if the other gentlemen don't mind.'

'Right now?'

'If it's convenient. It shouldn't take more than ten minutes.'

Sandu Stoicescu picked up a thick envelope from the coffee table in front of him and headed towards the kitchen. The President gave an embarrassed smile to the other three advisers, and followed him.

'Really, Sandu, wasn't that a bit over the top?'

'I'm fed up with their lies and tricks, sir. Your security adviser and Calin dream of nothing else but replacing the Minister of the Interior, so that they can muck around as they please with the border guards and the police corruption commission. The Minister has been loyal to you, he's competent, he's never plotted with others against you. You may not want to fire these advisers, but it doesn't seem fair to fire the guy who was merely doing his job.'

'Hush now, he's got his flaws as well.'

'Regarding the Sword case? That he didn't give in to the demands of your security adviser?'

'For example.'

'Even if those demands were illegal?'

'OK, stop giving me lessons in ethics. You've been in power long enough to know how the game is played. You have to fulfil certain demands, or else the system breaks down and we lose the election. Anyway, let me hear what you have to say about evidence.'

'I was the one who provided him with the evidence, so I know for sure he has it, sir.'

Stoicescu handed the contents of the envelope to the President, who leafed through them, then turned back to the first page and reread it more carefully.

'Excellent proof. But what are we going to do with it? We can't publicise it, can we?'

'Only if it's strictly necessary. Although that does mean I would probably have to resign.'

'So why did you give this to the Minister?'

'I didn't actually give him the material as such, I merely informed him of its contents. I can give it to him if you like.'

'No, no, that would lead to a huge scandal. You're going to be in trouble.'

'That's OK. I can take full responsibility for it. You didn't know anything about this material until after the Minister received it.'

'And what are we going to tell the guys next door?'

'We can tell them just a small part of the truth. And mainly to Marinescu, because he's our media guy.'

'Fine, but please try to stop them jumping at each other's throats. I've had enough of their fighting.'

When they returned to the dining room, there were only two of the men there. The security adviser had gone outside for a breath of fresh air.

'According to the documents that Stoicescu has shown me, we have enough here to put some pressure on the journalist Cornel Ardeleanu, who has betrayed us.'

'But, sir, did you see what he wrote in today's papers?'

'What did he write?'

'About the imminent conflict between Romanians and gypsies. He refers to a formal sociological study, conducted by several academics, which comes to the conclusion that the government's inaction, coupled with the general tendency of Romanian society to persecute minorities, will inevitably lead to a major bust-up between Romanians and gypsies. They also conducted an opinion poll which shows that seventy per cent of citizens believe that the government is responsible for the escalation of tension between ethnic groups.'

'Ha, our dear friend Cornel works hard for his money...'

'To be fair, I don't think that our gypsy friends read the papers too much, so it won't make them come out on the streets to protest.'

'It's not them I'm worried about. It's the foreign powers. First France Presse, now Cornel Ardeleanu claiming that interethnic conflict is imminent. Add to that the unfortunate incident with the dead child. Enough! If we get labelled the nasty party, we won't be able to get rid of that tag for a decade or more. Bastards!'

'All is fair in love and war, Mr President.'

'We have to find something to strike back. It's not enough to ask Cornel to stop this backstabbing. We have to find something to hit Rădulescu and Nenişor as well...'

'We might have something, sir,' Calin paused for dramatic effect and readjusted his position in the armchair. 'I've found Rădulescu's mother.'

'So what?'

'His birth mother, I mean, not the one who raised him. His real mother is a gypsy. She no longer leads a traveller lifestyle, she's getting too old now, but she did travel for a very long time. She now lives in abject poverty in Turnu Măgurele. I have all the details.'

'Do we really want to strike such a low blow? Go for the family?'

'You decide. But I believe that this kind of revelation would explain why Rădulescu and Nenişor are so close, and why he supports the gypsies so much. It might not be pretty, but it could get the public on our side. It might be the only good thing to come out of this whole Sword affair.'

The President spotted his security adviser pacing up and down in the courtyard. He hastily approved the matter and left the three of them to plan how to deal with it. Then he put on a jumper and went outside to reconcile with his adviser.

30

Beetle had always been the terror of his neighbourhood. He'd become notorious aged eight or nine, when he towered above the other children in the slums. His fist was leaden and his thirst for getting into fights was legendary. He liked punching and kicking, he enjoyed seeing beaten-up faces, with blood gushing from mouth and nose, he loved seeing the fear in their eyes. He might have been younger than most of the others, but he was used to getting his own way, because no-one wanted to get on the wrong side of him.

One time a boy who was ten years older than him, Pirtea, had mocked him, and he hadn't dared to do anything about it, because Pirtea was as big as a house and handy with a knife. Beetle let him be, bided his time. One night, when Pirtea came home drunk as a skunk, Beetle took the metal chain which was supposed to fence off the green space in front of the block of flats and beat him unconscious. They took the older boy away in an ambulance but couldn't save his eye. Of course, Pirtea never found out who'd done this to him, and Beetle was careful not to boast about it, although he'd have loved to.

His nickname was Beetle because he used to carry a matchbox with a shiny stag beetle inside. He would play with it while talking to others, let it crawl up his hand, move it from one palm to the other, get it to climb up to his wrist. If the other person annoyed him, Beetle would crush the stag beetle with one noisy crunch and wipe his hand all over their face or clothes. Then the real fight would start…

But then – disaster. At the age of thirteen or thereabouts, he stopped growing. One by one, all the other wide boys in the neighbourhood overtook him, and he stayed small and dark, like his beetles. He wasn't terribly smart either, struggling to finish primary school and dropping out after two years of secondary school. He continued to be extremely violent and prone to getting into fights, but in recent years he'd started getting beaten up. The others were either far bigger than him, or else they'd learnt martial arts or other fancy stuff. He'd only been to prison once, for a year, for a minor offence, and became part of a tough gang when he came out. Not that he had much to do, but the boss liked his crazy unpredictability, and would send him occasionally to scare people.

He was trying to shake the nickname Beetle, but everybody knew him by that name. And he did look like one.

He was wandering through the neighbourhood that afternoon, hands in his pockets. He didn't have anything to do, but he liked passing by the boss's bar to see if there was any small job for him. Usually there wasn't, but he would have a few drinks with the

SWORD

lads or play a round of billiards. For a brief moment, he had the feeling someone was following him. He looked behind him. No-one was there. He turned around suddenly. Still no one. He must be mistaken, but he couldn't shake that feeling of being watched. Who would want to stalk him, though, he was so unimportant? He crossed the street and then he saw something that froze his blood. A tall man, with a light grey trench-coat, his face half-covered by a scarf, holding something underneath his coat. Sword?

He sped up, gearing himself to run away. He was a gypsy and a criminal, so… The street was full of people, it was still light, although it was late November. He almost ran down the alleyway where the boss's bar was located. He thought there was no-one behind him, but he couldn't be sure.

He opened the door, rushed past the grumpy waitress who never greeted him, and went into the boss's office. He told the guys that he had been followed by Sword, that he was probably still somewhere outside. At first, they stared at him in disbelief – nobody gave much credit to whatever Beetle said – but finally a group of about seven of them ran out on the street. There was nobody outside.

They went to the intersection but there was no-one there fitting the description. Beetle then spotted the man heading towards the four-storey blocks of flats behind the pharmacy. They ran after him and attacked. They pushed him to the ground and started punching and kicking him.

The boss managed to stop them from using their knives to finish off the job. They opened up his trench coat, which was already covered in blood. Instead of a sword, they found a document tube, slightly bent out of shape from the fight. Beetle looked at the man in the trench-coat a bit more closely and realised that he knew him. It was a student who occasionally bought some weed from him. He looked a bit drugged up even now. But at least he was still breathing…

The boss told them all to scram from there, and hoped that no one had seen them. But even if they had, who would speak up for a pathetic little druggie?

31

Cornel Ardeleanu's office was small and cramped, with lots of posters on the walls. Instead of a PC, he had an old-fashioned typewriter on his desk. He refused to type his editorials on anything else. In fact, he was dead set against computers or any other technological advances. He had started his journalistic careers typing on a Remington that his grandfather's friend had brought back from Austria. It had been adapted for Romanian letters and it had been avidly used for half a century. He'd used it during Ceaușescu's era, and he wasn't planning to stop using it now. Of course, back in those days he'd had to declare it to the police, but it had travelled all over the world with him. After his second divorce, it had been one of the few things he'd kept, aside from a few clothes and books.

Marinescu was patiently listening to the epic story of Cornel's typewriter, which he'd heard at least four times before. He had been served some tea, but it was incredibly bitter, and there was never any sugar in Ardeleanu's office, so he gave up trying to drink it. He set down the teacup on the little coffee table full of pictures, envelopes, files, papers. On a previous visit, when Ardeleanu had started writing an urgent newsflash, and Marinescu had been bored out of his mind, he'd tried to sneak a peek at some of the pictures. But Ardeleanu caught him at it and started yelling that these things were personal and no one was allowed to see them.

There was another envelope full of pictures right in front of Marinescu right now, but he didn't even bother glancing at it. He had enough to discuss with the journalist.

'So, the old man is cross with me?' Ardeleanu couldn't resist teasing his friend.

'He is, rather.'

'See, this is the beauty of this job, mate. You can do as you please, it doesn't matter if he's the President. Only half the country voted for him. I told him off because I think he was wrong. And nobody can do anything about it. Because I can't be bought off. I have everything I need. A few weeks ago, Radu Rădulescu came to see me – sitting in that very chair you're sitting in now. He was silent, I was silent. He made some small talk, I made some small talk. And then, at some point, he finally said: "I know what's the problem with you, Ardeleanu. You don't need anything from anyone. If you feel like it, you attack someone; if not, you don't. No one can convince you to do otherwise." You see, pal, Rădulescu understands me. Maybe he's not so stupid after all.'

Ardeleanu fell silent, seemingly lost in thought. After a minute or so, he asked: 'So, why are you here? Do you want something from me?'

'Not necessarily, Cornel.'

'Oh, come off it, mate! I bet the President sent you to yell at me. Why couldn't he just call me directly? Like he used to do before he became President? See? Power corrupts. When he needed me, he used to call. Now he just sends his ... advisers.'

'Just say it: his underlings. I don't mind. That's what you called us in your article. At least I'm the underling of a man I respect and believe in. Whose underling are you?'

'Oi, don't you start...'

'Cornel, we know very well that you took money from Rădulescu to run a hostile campaign against the President. In fact, we have proof.'

Marinescu took one of the two green folders he had brought with him and handed it to his old mate. Ardeleanu opened it, looked at the first page, reddened and started shouting.

'You've had me under surveillance, you bastards! You're tapping my phones! I will destroy you. I will get the entire press to destroy you. How dare you come and threaten me like this? Get out!'

'Before I get out, allow me to advise you to read things more carefully. You might notice that it wasn't you who was under surveillance, but the other guy. The guy who paid you is an arms dealer and the Prosecution Service has approved close surveillance for him, including phone tapping. We acted therefore perfectly legally. What is also clear, however, is that you were bribed. What will the German owners of your paper say when they find out you took money from a known arms dealer to attack the sitting President? Yes, the President may lose the next election, but you stand to lose so much more: your reputation, your job, your social status. Have you earned enough money from bribes to be able to retire at forty-four? Am I making myself clear or do you still want me to get out?'

Ardeleanu sat back down in his chair and mumbled something.

'Fine. Now, you have here another folder, with some interesting facts about Rădulescu. Or rather, about his family. We would be delighted if you would publish an article – better still, a series of articles – about this matter, not forgetting one of your incisive editorials. OK? And, just to show you that we're not the baddies around here, we'll send you someone from the Privatisation Fund to write up a contract for advertising with you. You decide how much – but don't go wild. You can decide how much you want to pass on to your Germans or keep for yourself. Oh, and "mate"? Don't take it personally. We do love you, you know.'

32

Cotroceni Park was eerie and drained of colour in early winter. The only way to describe the landscape you could see from the windows of the President's study would be like something out of the poet Bacovia's work: dead leaves, denuded trees, mud and mire, enlivened only by a crow croaking every now and then from the top of a tree.

The President was tired and feeling rather ill after attending the military parade to celebrate the 1st of December National Holiday. He'd laid the wreath at the Tomb of the Unknown Soldier. It was terribly draughty there and he'd made the mistake of braving the rain without a hat on his head, to avoid being unfavourably compared to his predecessor. He'd started sneezing during the parade and, although he'd been given hot tea and aspirin behind the scenes, he was sure he was coming down with a cold. He swallowed another fistful of pills, sipped his tea, and asked his chief of staff to let the two guests in. They were the directors of the largest polling institute in Bucharest, and they'd been waiting outside for twenty-five minutes. They came in and presented their latest opinion poll results.

'So Rădulescu's party is ten points in the lead? And his party says that all they need is twelve per cent to be assured of election victory. We are well and truly screwed.'

'What's even worse, sir, is that there is a downward tendency as far as you are concerned. If you can't make a dramatic change, then you will continue to slide down in the public esteem.'

'What dramatic change? This is going to be the harshest winter in twenty years. The World Bank is likely to refuse to give us another loan. Every single bloody day I seem to have one union or another going on strike. As well as this madness about the gypsies.'

'It has to be said that when you ask people open questions, no one seems particularly interested in the Sword case anymore. Only about eight per cent mentioned it. The others are far more concerned about unemployment, healthcare, prices, corruption, inflation, government indecision … in roughly that order.'

'Well, it continues to be a problem for me. Did you ask them how they feel about the Roma minority?'

'I did. Sixty-five per cent have a bad or very bad opinion about this ethnic group and eighty-five per cent of them would rather not live in neighbourhoods where there is a large Roma population. There is even a dangerous proportion of Romanians - eighteen to twenty per cent - who see violence as the only solution to the Roma problem. And that's dangerous.'

'So why is Rădulescu's popularity soaring?'

'It's not popularity. The only reason he is going up is because you are going down. The votes you are losing are transferring to him.'

'Do you think it would make a difference if people found out that he's a gypsy?'

'Who is?'

'Rădulescu. Would this change things?'

'But is he really?'

'Yes, he is. I believe that Ardeleanu has unearthed some documents about his family, which prove that he is a gypsy.'

'Hmm … not sure. It could matter in some instances, given that it is the most senior position in the country. But it probably wouldn't be a lethal blow. Do you want me to check?'

'Let's wait for this to be publicised and then you can conduct another poll.'

'And what do you want us to do with the current one?'

'We need to change a couple of things. I'm not sure how to word it regarding the Sword situation – maybe make it clear that the people are not happy with the politicisation of this case.'

'How are we going to make that clear?'

'Maybe ask the question: "Do you agree with the way Rădulescu is trying to politicise the situation?"'

'We can't do that – it's unprofessional.'

'Well, what question can we ask?'

'We could ask who is to blame for the case remaining unsolved…'

'That's a stupid question: it's clear that it's the Minister of the Interior who is to blame, therefore indirectly the President. When you're at the top, you're the one to blame for everything. No point in asking this question at all! The problem is not the case itself, but the fact that they are using it as a political football. Rădulescu and his sidekick Nenișor want to transform this police matter into an interethnic conflict which will damage my credibility abroad and destabilise me inside the country. That's exactly what I am trying to fight against. You yourself told me there was no trace of interethnic conflict.'

'That's not what we said. We said that the public doesn't consider the Sword issue to be terribly important. It's not their top priority. But it is a well-known case and there are indeed tensions between Romanians and Romas. I told you that twenty per cent of Romanians agree that violent methods are necessary against the Romas – so in essence, they agree with the assassin. At any given moment, some of these aggressive twenty per cent of people might decide to copy what the killer is doing.'

'Well, that's one conclusion you can't publish by any means! Be careful – the international press has started reporting on the case as well. Mostly taking on board what our wonderful journalists are saying, without any critical reasoning. I sometimes wonder what would happen if I left the country in their "capable" hands: Rădulescu, Nenișor and all those journalists. Let them sort things out!'

The phone rang but the President didn't answer. A few moments later his chief of staff came into the office and said there was an important message for him. A man had been found with his throat cut behind the station in the port town of Constanţa. The victim was a notorious pimp named Aurel Coaja. He reported that the Minister of the Interior had begun organising checkpoints on all the roads and railways, because if the killer was Sword, he would come back to Bucharest. They were also checking all the hotels by the coast. The MO appeared very similar to the previous murders.

The President bid the pollsters goodbye. Then he asked his chief of staff to get hold of Marinescu.

'But it's a holiday...'

'So what? I'm in the office, aren't I? He can come in too. Send a car for him.'

'It's just that when it's a holiday, Marinescu starts drinking quite early in the morning. By now he must be completely blotto. I doubt we'd be able to wake him up.'

The President sat frowning, deep in thought. He asked his chief of staff to give the opinion poll results to one of his advisers to massage the figures a bit.

'I want Rădulescu to appear lower and myself higher. He should only track two per cent above me. And I don't want anything about Sword to appear there. That question about trust – do you trust that Romania is heading in the right direction – I want forty-five per cent to say yes, thirty-five no, and the rest don't know. And tomorrow, when Marinescu gets in, tell him to write me a major speech. Something like a state of the nation. I need to give them all a slap in the face.'

33

Captain Andronescu had deployed his three riot control units two hours ago. They'd been on emergency standby since early in the morning, when it was announced that the police in Constanţa had arrested a suspect in the Sword case. He had placed his men in front of the police station and flanking either side of the building to supervise the gathering crowds of gypsies massing in the little square outside the main police station and spilling out into the adjoining streets. There were about two hundred of them, all still relatively calm. He'd tried to go up to talk to a few of them, but they moved away and rejoined the crowds somewhere else.

He radioed his superior officers about the strange lull that seemed to reign around him. The Romas seemed to be well organised and waiting for something, perhaps for a sign. He stepped back inside to drink a coffee and warm up a little. It was not quite below zero outside, but the wind was blowing in from the sea in fierce, damp squalls. He asked the duty chief of station why he wasn't communicating with the people outside, but he was told that they were waiting for a message from the mayor. Half an hour later, the message finally arrived and the duty chief, accompanied by two other officers, went outside to address the crowds. Andronescu did not follow them.

Suddenly, he heard shouting and booing coming from outside. He gave a quick order and the front line of riot police rushed to the aid of the officers surrounded by gypsies. Using their batons and plastic shields, they managed to extricate the officers. The gypsies tried to attack them again, and Andronescu sent forward the second row of policemen. It was a free-for-all, but the superior training and equipment of the police stood them in good stead. They managed to return to the police station intact, having arrested ten of the more violent gypsies. The duty chief had received a punch to the face, three other officers had minor injuries. The ten gypsies were taken to the basement cells for questioning.

Andronescu called for reinforcements. The crowds had recovered from the initial shock and were surging forward again. The riot police stopped them with their batons and shields and threw smoke grenades. The duty chief was urging Andronescu to get his units to counterattack while the gypsies were overcome by smoke, but Andronescu preferred to wait for reinforcements. After all, you could never be too sure how many people were out there in the streets beyond the square.

The wind quickly dispersed the fumes. The gypsies had improvised face masks with their scarves or handkerchiefs and were ready to attack once more.

A two-pronged attack, from the front and sides. The police easily withstood the frontal attack, but they were nearly overcome on the flanks. They had to use smoke grenades once more. Andronescu could see the fear in the eyes of some of his men, and still there were no reinforcements. He asked for permission to use firearms, but he was told no, help was on its way and they should hold out just a little longer.

The crowds were throwing stones and broken bottles at them. Meanwhile, the police were responding with smoke grenades and tear gas. The wind had dropped, so the tear gas was wafting throughout the square. There was another avalanche of stones and bottles, and the gypsies surged forward howling and swearing. Then – finally! – Andronescu saw additional riot police running up towards the square from two side streets.

He took off his mask and bellowed an order to attack. The Romas were now caught in a pincer movement between the two flanks of the riot squad. Red-eyed from the gas and caught by surprise, they started to run and disperse, while more and more policemen were making their appearance on all the side streets. By the time the armoured vehicles arrived, Andronescu had stood down all but the front line of his units.

Then, suddenly, there was a new wave of rocks and bottles being thrown on the left-hand side of the square, which had not suffered any attacks previously. Some of the bottles were Molotov cocktails, and one of them set a tree alight. Another hit a policeman and set light to his uniform. He screamed and fell to the ground, rolling. Andronescu took off his jacket and flung himself onto the man, using his jacket like a blanket to try and quench the flames, which had spread to the young man's hair. Two officers ran up with a fire extinguisher (which didn't work) and a sand bucket.

The young man stopped screaming. They finally managed to put out the fire, but they could no longer feel his pulse. When the ambulance arrived, the paramedics declared him dead.

The riot in the square was by now fully under control. Many of the rioters had been arrested, others were being pursued in the surrounding streets.

34

'Good evening, ladies and gentlemen, we are interrupting our normal programme for some breaking news, brought to you by Irina Lascar.'

'Good evening. There have been violent clashes between the police forces and several hundred Romas in Constanţa earlier today. As a result of the street fights, one policeman has died and several people were injured. We are going over to our special correspondent Dan Dumitrescu. What can you tell us, Dan?'

'What can I say? The events took place a couple of hours ago and have been described as one of the most violent scenes of the post-revolutionary era. Around three hundred and fifty Romas clashed with the police forces here. The reason appears to be that the local paper reported that a suspect had been arrested in the Sword case, whose latest victim had been Aurel Coaja, a notorious local gangster. Multiple gypsy clans gathered in front of the police station to demand justice. In actual fact, no suspect was being held in custody at that police station. The duty chief of police went out to tell them that there was no suspect, that the paper had reported fake news. He even offered to show the leaders around the police station, so that they could establish for themselves that there was no Sword being held there. Instead of listening, however, the gypsy clans attempted to take a police officer hostage, so the riot police had to intervene. That's how the conflict escalated. It led to the tragic death of young Constable Horia Sârbu, who was only twenty years old. He was injured when a Molotov cocktail hit him. His colleagues were unable to save him. At the moment, there are over one hundred Romas in custody. Meanwhile, thirty police officers and seventy Romas are being treated for their injuries, but none of them are in a critical condition.'

'Thank you, Dan. We've invited the Minister of the Interior onto our programme to discuss this matter in more depth. Good evening. What is the current situation?'

'Everything is under control now, just like your correspondent said. We are currently questioning over one hundred people and will soon get to the bottom of the matter as to who instigated the riot, and who threw the petrol bomb which killed officer Sârbu. At the same time, I would like to emphasise that we are also investigating the journalist who wrote the false piece of news which led to this tragic event.'

'Do you consider him guilty?'

'Irina, it was a simple matter to fact check the information. The police had taken no less than six suspects in for questioning following the murder of Aurel Coaja, but none of them were being held at the main police station, and furthermore all of them had already been released after questioning. There was no lack of transparency on the part of the police. They had released a statement to that effect the previous night. The police acted quickly and efficiently. The only thing that could have provoked such a riot was that erroneous article published in the paper. What I want to know is this: was simply a stupid mistake or was it deliberate? Because, sadly, a promising young man, barely fresh out of school, died as a result of it.'

'Do you think this incident will lead to an escalation of interethnic conflict?'

'Maybe you should ask MP Nenişor Vasile about this. He's been pushing the Roma population to take revenge for months. Well, now he's got what he wanted: bloodshed. He has that poor burnt boy on his conscience. My advisers have told me I shouldn't be so brutally honest about this, but they haven't seen that poor boy's corpse. I have. I can no longer stay calm and say nothing. Because this is yet again an example of how the innocent pay for all that is wrong in this country. I take my share of the blame, me and the police, for failing to capture this serial killer. But I consider that the politicians are even more to blame, using interethnic conflict to drive their polling figures up. And it's innocents like Sârbu who are dead, not Nenişor, not Radu Rădulescu, not even me or the journalist who published the fake news.'

'You seem very upset by it all, minister…'

'Yes, I am. I've been in touch with his family and have let them know, but I also want to take this opportunity to announce publicly that officer Sârbu has been posthumously promoted to Sergeant and his family will receive a full police pension.'

'What next?'

'If I hadn't made it my personal mission to catch this murderer, I would be ready to announce my resignation here on air. But first I feel compelled to catch him, and then I will resign.'

'But why? That's not the usual thing to do.'

'Because I believe we have to maintain some dignity and honour in our political life.'

'I completely understand, Minister. Thank you. Ladies and gentlemen, we will be back with the latest updates in our usual news bulletin.'

After they left the studio, Irina congratulated the Minister on his excellent interview. As soon as he left the TV station, he called his adviser.

'See, didn't I tell you they'd lap it up? That was the right tone to take. See you back in the office in half an hour.'

35

Reporter Dan Dumitrescu woke up with a severe hangover, after a heavy bout of drinking the night before with his friends from Constanța. He couldn't remember much about where they'd gone, what they'd done, or how he'd made his way back to his hotel room. All he knew was that this morning he was supposed to be in the village of Movileni, somewhere near Buzău, more than two hundred kilometres from Constanța, to report live from the funeral of that unfortunate young policeman who'd been burnt alive. Luckily, he'd sent his cameraman ahead the previous day with the little TV van. His plan was to rent a car and drive there himself. He'd been a reporter for eleven years, had covered all the major conflicts in Yugoslavia, Transnistria, Chechnya, the Gulf, Angola, Somalia and Palestine. He had seen more death and misery than any sane human being could handle in a single lifetime. But the truth was, he couldn't imagine himself doing anything else.

On the way to the funeral, he got a flat tyre. To his astonishment, the rental car didn't have a spare tyre, so he had to hitchhike to the nearest garage with the tyre on his lap and then hitchhike all the way back to the car again, to replace it. Luckily, it was dry and sunny, though frosty, so there were plenty of cars on the road to give him a lift.

The cameraman had been calling him with increasing desperation, because he had no idea what to do on his own. He'd only been working in TV for six months, and worried constantly about making any mistakes. Dan decided to stop taking his calls.

He finally got to the village at three in the afternoon. The cameraman had told him that the cemetery was at the other end of the village, while the house of the dead policeman's family was on the main street leading up to the cemetery. The village seemed very peaceful. There was nobody around, except for two children holding hands to cross the road, followed by a little white dog. The houses were neat and tidy, almost every one of them had a car parked in the front. Dacias, nothing grander, but still. It showed the people in this village were relatively well-off, raising animals, growing vegetables. He drove past the sharp bend that he'd been warned about by at least three different traffic signs, passed by a pond with three fishermen sitting on its banks, overtook a lorry parked pretty much in the middle of the road and stopped in front of the village shop and the school.

That's when he first saw the clouds of smoke. On the right-hand side of the road he could see columns of smoke rising and flames flickering between the trees. He lowered his window and heard yelling and crying. He restarted his car and turned right to go towards the smoke, but a row of policemen blocked his way. He showed them his press pass, but they refused to let him through. He parked his car and tried to make his way there on foot, but he was stopped once more. What was going on?

The policeman's family had decided to take revenge on the few gypsy families living in their village. They had set fire to their homes and were trying to find and kill all the family members. The police were there to keep the rest of the villagers away from the incident, but in fact no one seemed keen to get any closer to the conflict. They preferred to watch from a safe distance, above the heads of the police cordon. Some children had climbed up trees for a better view.

Dan found the officer in charge, showed him his press pass and managed to get through. He found out that there were at least two people dead, and that no-one knew where his cameraman was.

The houses that had been set on fire were not on the main road, but tucked away, close to the fields surrounding the village. There was an acrid smell of burning and moans and cries coming from the houses; a couple were still in flames. Several gypsy women were sitting on the ground, gathering their voluminous skirts around them and crying. Two of them had faces covered in blood, another was having her arm bandaged by a police first-aider. The gypsy men, together with the police, were trying to douse the flames with buckets of water and sand. The fire engines from Buzau were delayed, so they had to make do with what was on hand. In front of the third smouldering ruin, Dan caught a glimpse of his cameraman at last. He was filming an elderly gypsy, who was telling the police how the intruders had stormed into his home, beaten up his son with a metal crowbar and then set fire to the house. The boy was next to him, smoke-blackened and with an ugly bruise already forming on his forehead.

Another cameraman had had his equipment smashed to smithereens. The young policeman's family were not only angry with the gypsies but also with any and all journalists. They'd set fire to four houses in that part of the village, and to another one just beyond the cemetery. Apparently, there were six dead: one man stabbed in the café, three or four beaten up and one or two who died in the fire.

The policeman who had died had four older brothers, who all worked elsewhere, Buzău, Brăila, Bucharest. They had all come home for the funeral with a few of their beefier mates from work. They'd done a recce the evening before and the massacre had started this morning.

By chance, the local prefect had sent a police squad to the village that day, because there had been rumours that one or two senior government officials might attend the funeral. Once the violence had started, several more units had made their appearance. Several of the aggressors had been arrested, while others were being held in the deceased police officer's parental home.

Dan approached the fourth house. They'd managed to extinguish the flames, but it was still smouldering.

SWORD

In front of the entrance, he saw a dog probably beaten to death with crow bars. Its head was smashed open, but you could still see the trusting, pleading eyes. The policemen had stepped on him twice already in their frantic scramble to pour sand. Dan looked at the poor blood-drenched creature covered in mud and ashes. He shuddered, then took out his microphone and went in to do his job.

36

The President entered the reception room at Cotroceni Palace, accompanied by his national security adviser. The German ambassador was waiting for him. He was on his own, without even an interpreter. He had, after all, been born in Romania and had spent his childhood here, so there weren't any communication problems. The President thanked him for the generous donations that the ambassador and other embassy staff had made for the victims of the autumn floods in Transylvania. It was good to see that Europe, and Germany in particular, stood side-by-side with Romania in its most difficult moments.

The ambassador in turn thanked the President for his help in resolving the delicate issue with the lease on the current embassy building and for granting them a piece of land on which they could build a new embassy.

The President then asked about the German Chancellor's plans for her upcoming visit to Romania just before the OSCE Summit.

'That's precisely what I wanted to talk to you about, Mr President. I was told this very morning that the

Chancellor can no longer come to Romania and will be sending the Deputy Minister of Foreign Affairs instead.'

'But it's been in her calendar for a very long time. I spoke to her on the phone a month ago and she confirmed our agenda for discussion.'

'That's right, but recent events have led us to believe that it might be wiser to reschedule the visit. It wasn't a state visit anyway, merely a side visit to the OSCE Summit.'

'I'm afraid, Your Excellency, you will have to be a bit clearer than that. What recent events are you referring to? Any international or bilateral events?'

'No, simply that public opinion in Germany and of course the federal government are concerned about the worsening situation regarding security in your country. The interethnic conflict which took place two days ago just outside Buzău has got us all worried. We are convinced that Romania will act firmly and promptly to avoid the escalation of such conflicts in future. Europe, and the Balkans in particular, cannot afford to become another interethnic battleground.'

'Your Excellency, let me leave diplomatic language aside for a minute and be perfectly candid with you. The major problem that Romania has faced since 1989 is that it is being marginalised within Europe. At first we were told that this was because those in power were still the old communists. They accused them of not respecting human rights, lack of democracy, lack of freedom of expression, state corruption and so on. Then we got elected,' the President said. 'Europe had consistently told us that they wanted somebody like us. All our European contacts had told us before the elections that they would lend us their support so that we could finally get through this transition period. That's what we told the electorate and they believed us. But after we got voted in, new criteria popped up. There were no anti-democratic developments, there was no lack of freedom of speech. Instead we now got measured according to various economic criteria. We embarked upon a painful economic reform, which cost us virtually all of our popularity. A large part of our population fell into nearly unacceptable levels of poverty, but we bit our lip and carried on as instructed. Now you come up with the criteria for ethnic integration. Well, if that is the case, why do you send our Romas packing every time you stumble across them in Germany? If you consider that they are committing crimes and causing social instability in your country, don't you think they might be causing the same problems here? Aren't you carrying out ethnic cleansing in your country? Why is it only called interethnic aggression when it happens here? In the village you're referring to, it was a conflict between some Roma families and a Romanian family whose son had just been killed by Romas. The perpetrators have been arrested and will face trial. Our public services have done their jobs. And the conflict was about social matters, not ethnic ones.'

'Thank you for your honesty, but you have to understand that such clashes are a great source of anxiety in Europe and the rest of the world.'

'Stop sending us to the back of the queue. Invest in Romania and such incidents will disappear. The more you continue to delay our European integration, the more poverty we experience and the greater the spike in social tensions. And anti-European sentiments, I might add. When I first got elected, ninety per cent of Romanians were in favour of the EU, the highest rate in Eastern Europe. Now it's around fifty-five to sixty per cent. Ask yourselves why. But first, I would like you to ask the Chancellor to come to Bucharest as we agreed, because later on such a visit might become pointless.'

'Is that really what you want me to say?'

'Actually, I will tell her myself on the phone. Romania has done nothing wrong. The way the situation is being presented abroad gives the false impression that Romania and its government are to blame. But that is wrong. The situation is completely under control.'

37

The Grand Hall of the National Theatre was packed with people from all over the country. All around the hall, there were name plates for each of the forty counties of Romania. While the attendees were taking their places, young people dressed in black milled around, carrying national flags as well as the black-and-white flag of the National Unity Movement. The loudspeakers were booming with the party anthem 'We are Romanians'. The stage was decorated in the National Unity colours of black and white, and featured a projection of the NUM's symbol, an eagle with swords in its talons.

The NUM's vice-presidents walked out on the stage to the applause of all present, and stood on either side of the podium, waiting for their party leader, Theodor Varlaam. He made a flamboyant and noisy entry at the back of the hall, surrounded by eight statuesque young men clad, naturally, in black. He walked all the way to the front among the rows of attendees, who were all standing and clapping frenetically. Once on stage, he asked them all to stand – which they were doing anyway – for the national anthem. Afterwards, he asked a priest to recite 'Our Father' and bless every one of them. After the final amen, they all sat down and Varlaam could begin.

'Welcome to the annual conference of the most important party in Romania, the National Unity Movement. '

That was enough to get the public to stand once more amidst wild applause. Varlaam let them enjoy themselves for a minute or two before continuing.

'It's the most important party, not just because we have the highest number of members, nor because we have the most active branches throughout the country. It's the most important not just because we always do very well at the real polls, not those fake ones commissioned by the corrupt government. No, our party is the most important one because it is the only one that is truly Romanian in spirit. The only party that doesn't beg for a scrap of attention from either the West or the East. It has only one true master: the Romanian people. At every election, we've been robbed by those without roots or without God, who aim to please foreign masters. But this year we will emerge victorious! Romanians can no longer stand feeling like second-class citizens in their own country. They have been crying in silence for far too long. I tell you now: stop crying, grab hold of your anger, unite under the flag of our Movement and topple this traitorous government! Chase away all those who have sold off our country! Everywhere we turn in this country, things are in the hands of foreigners. We no longer eat Romanian bread – no, our bread is Turkish, while our golden wheat rots in the fields. We no longer eat Romanian chicken, we eat Hungarian ones, while our poultry dies of hunger in abandoned battery farms. Ten years ago we were exporting industrial equipment all over the world, but nowadays the world powers tell us to close down our factories and make our people unemployed, or else send them abroad to work for them in slave conditions.

'We Romanians have throughout history known how to resist all sorts of foreign invasions: Attila the Hun, Arpad the Hungarian, Mehmed the Conqueror, Sobieski the saviour of Vienna, the German troops of Mackensen, Stalin's Russians… But if we don't unite now, then Romania is in grave danger. Our agriculture, which has sustained us for so many centuries and which made us the granary of Europe, is now close to collapse. Our farmers now buy bread from the cities – Turkish bread. Our industry, which allowed us to be independent, has now been sold off to foreign companies at risible prices and deliberately dismantled. Our proud culture, which produced the likes of Brancusi, Enescu, Eliade, Tristan Tzara and above all Eminescu, is now suffocated by cheap commercial film imports from the US or vulgar music from Turkish and gypsy sub-cultures.

'Our youth is leaving the country in droves to work in humiliating jobs abroad, or to fight as mercenaries under foreign flags. Our young women are driven by poverty and despair to walk the streets of Istanbul, Cyprus or Athens. We've left Bessarabia in the hands of the Russians, and Bucovina in the hands of the Ukrainians. Southern Dobrogea is now Bulgarian, and Transylvania is slowly but surely reverting to Hungary, with the complicity of the current government.

'There is a conspiracy afoot in the West to carve up Romania – and nobody is coming to our rescue. Our only chance is to regroup once more under the spear of Iron Guard leader Horia Sima. He had faith in the strength of this nation, in its ability to withstand foreign invaders for so many centuries. But we also need to learn to guard against traitors from within. While we stand guard at our borders, these rats are spreading poison inside the country. But the National Unity Movement has unmasked them and no one trusts them anymore. The revolution is nigh!

'That traitor of a President and his mercenary advisers and foreign agents are hiding on the hill of Cotroceni, but I tell them: midnight is approaching! The clock is striking! And the dawn of a new world will arise for all. For the miner who has watched his mine close and is now begging for a scrap of bread. For the farmer who gets no subsidy at all from the state. For the humiliated officer who's been kicked out of the army at the request of a foreign power. For the Orthodox priest who barely has room in his own country because of the onslaught of neo-Protestant sects swarming in. For the honest pensioner who after forty years of hard work sees that he hasn't got enough money to survive beyond tomorrow. For years, we believed that it was merely a war of words between political parties – that underneath it all, we were all patriots who wanted what's best for the country. But I was wrong!

'Words are no longer enough. We need to take action. We need to get justice for ourselves with all the righteous anger of Avram Iancu and the determination of Vlad Țepeș. What do you think will happen to the criminals who killed that poor policeman in Constanța? Nothing! They have probably been released already. Because gypsies are protected by Europe, they want to make Romania a gypsy ghetto, just as they wanted to make Moldova a Jewish ghetto once upon a time. During Antonescu's time, if someone killed a Romanian soldier, they would be hung on the spot. But now, on the tomb of young Horia Sârbu, burnt alive in the course of fulfilling his duties, politicians are having long debates about human rights. What about our rights, who is going to protect those? Our women who are raped by gypsies? Our children bullied and beaten up at school? Our grandparents and parents being robbed? Nobody protects them. Because the Romanian state only cares about gypsies, Turks, Hungarians, Arabs and everyone but the Romanians. So it's time to take action. Go beyond the political struggle and declare an open battle.

'I thereby declare Horia Sârbu, the policeman murdered in such horrific circumstances, to be a national hero. And I declare Sword to be an honorary member of the National Unity Movement. What tribunal and what judge would dare to condemn this fearless fighter for our rights, when the corrupt courts and police forces fail to protect us? Sword is courageous... and this is the way to clean up Romania!'

38

It was Saturday afternoon and the department store was heaving with shoppers. Christmas was fast approaching. Marcel was doing his rounds, checking that the store detectives and security guards were all in place, inspecting the CCTV cameras, doing a sweep of the car park at the back of the store. He'd been head of security for the department store for three years and he was very content with his status. Before arriving here, he'd been a martial arts instructor at various gyms, all of which had gone bust, one by one, then a bodyguard for a smartarse who was now in prison for smuggling offences. He had even been a police officer briefly, but this job was far more suited to him. He'd managed to solve many of the shop's problems, had convinced various gypsy clans not to bother them anymore, and had called a truce with most people, except for Titi Genocide. The problem with Genocide was that Marcel was the one who had arrested him back in his rookie police officer days, so the guy just couldn't forgive him. He kept sending pickpockets, currency fraudsters or beggars over to the store.

SWORD

Things had come to a head after the death of that fourteen-year-old who was a distant cousin of Titi's. Marcel had met with Genocide twice since the death of the boy, he'd met with the other clans, he'd explained that the whole thing had been a tragic accident, that his guards hadn't touched the boy, that he'd stumbled and fallen on his own. On top of that, Genocide had not kept his side of the bargain to not send pickpockets to the store, although the store owner was paying them all protection money. The other clans agreed with him, but you couldn't reason with Titi Genocide.

Marcel passed by the music section and smiled at Alina, his secret lover. He headed towards the car park. Once he finished his afternoon round, he could relax with his second cup of coffee and the sports section of the papers. Although he also had to convince the shop owner to give a bonus to the six specially trained security guards, whose skills were so impressive that they'd played a significant part in achieving a state of truce with the gypsy gangs.

All of a sudden, his walkie-talkie sparked into life. There was a problem at the main entrance. He ran down and saw three of his men in a face-off with around eleven giants, armed with bats and knives. Three more were approaching from the left-hand side, four more from the right. Two of his specially trained guards were there already, but he called the rest of them on his walkie-talkie immediately. He couldn't really count on his uniformed staff, they were there more for show. He joined the three men facing up to the intruders. He recognised a couple of the intruders as being Genocide's men, but he didn't know the others. They all seemed to be very calm, decisive and up for it.

The shoppers hadn't quite realised what was going on, but were giving the two groups of men a very wide berth.

Without warning, and with no visible signal, the eleven intruders rushed forward to attack Marcel and his men. Marcel punched the colossus in front of him in the throat, then headbutted him in the face and pushed him over. Another man attacked him with a knife. Marcel caught his hand and twisted it, but he was hit over the head with a chain, which left him momentarily blinded. He managed not to let go of the hand of the man with the knife, and pushed him in front as a sort of shield. He could see behind him one his guards being felled by an iron bar. The man with the chain was built like a fridge. He tried to hit Marcel once more, but hit the guy with the knife instead. Blood came gushing out. Marcel dropped him and jumped on the chain-wielder, punching him in the throat and headbutting him in the mouth.

His four back-ups had arrived and had already knocked out a broad-shouldered man who'd been swinging a metal bar and a man in a green hoodie waving a knife. Marcel was attacked by another two men trying to stab him with their knives. He managed to knock one of them to the ground, but the second cut him just above the elbow. He caught the man's arm and tried to break it, but the attacker was built like a tank and managed to escape unharmed. While he was still trying to make the first attacker drop his weapon, the other one came forward with a wielding a knife. In the confusion, he did not manage to plunge his knife into Marcel, but instead slashed his own mate in the belly.

Six of Genocide's men and three of the security guards were lying on the floor. Shoppers had fled from the area, and the sales assistants were hiding under their counters. Marcel kicked an intruder in the kidneys, while one of his guards felled another of them with a single blow. The others ran away, including the ones who had been waiting and watching on the left and right flank of the main area. The whole fight had lasted less than five minutes.

The police arrived soon after. There were no fatalities, but three of the aggressors and one of the guards were badly injured. Marcel had a pounding headache and a nasty bump where he'd been hit by the chain. He lay down flat on the floor, feeling faint. He would probably have to spend a couple of days in hospital. Alina, the sales assistant in the music section, held his hand while a paramedic bandaged his head. She was a lovely girl, but he really was getting too old for that sort of thing.

39

Ten days ago, in Constanța, we witnessed a battle between a few hundred gypsies and the police, in broad daylight, in the centre of town, in full view of all and sundry. Three days later, a dozen or so Romanians fought with a dozen or so gypsies in Movila, a village near Buz?u. Again, in broad daylight, in full view of all and sundry. Yesterday we witnessed a fracas between a dozen Romanians and twenty or so gypsies in a Bucharest department store. In broad daylight, in the centre of town, witnessed by all. A total of seven dead, a hundred injured, and serious damage to goods and property.

In four days' time, Bucharest will be hosting the OSCE Summit. The host, Romania, is a pillar of stability in the region, or so the government says. Because that is ALL the government says. It doesn't say a word about these violent scenes straight out of a Western – as if they weren't happening in our country, but somewhere far, far away, another time, another place, on CNN. The government's only reaction on this issue was to condemn Theodor Varlaam for the fiery speech he gave at his party conference, when he claimed there was a conflict between Romanians and Romas. There is no such conflict, the government maintains, Varlaam is trying to instigate hatred and violence.

If that's true, then where do those seven deaths come from? What has been going on these past ten days? How can you not be moved by the unbearably sad words uttered by the mother of the dead policeman? "I had six boys, whom I raised all on my own since my husband's death fifteen years ago. Now one of them is dead and the remaining five are in prison because of what happened in Movila. Am I the one to blame?" Is the government going to answer this simple question, coming from a dusty, forgotten corner of the country? Or do they only care about questions coming from NATO, the EU, a head of state or an important NGO?

Are we to blame? Maybe we are, for voting for you and giving you the power to punish us like this.

'This is Adrian Maier's front page editorial today. In fact, all the front pages are full of the confrontation at the department store in Bucharest. Typical headlines include: Blood and Violence in Bucharest; Romania on the Brink of Civil War; Police Counting Dead Bodies; Explosion of Violence in the Capital; Who's Going to Protect Us?

It's a hot topic and of course we are going to talk about it in tonight's show. Our guest is the well-known journalist and newspaper editor Cornel Ardeleanu. His paper published some unprecedented information about Radu R?dulescu's background today. If the opinion polls are right, R?dulescu is not only the leader of the largest opposition party, but potentially also the future President of Romania. So, Mr Ardeleanu, by publishing these personal details, one might say you've been helping the current government. If they lose the election despite all that, aren't you afraid that the current opposition will want their revenge against you?'

'Good evening, ladies and gentlemen, good evening, Mr Ivan. I've been in this job for twenty-five years and I'm no longer afraid of anything. All I did was publish the truth, regardless of how painful or inconvenient it might be for some. That's what being a journalist is all about...'

'You claim that R?dulescu's biological mother is in fact of Roma extraction. How did you find out all these spectacular details?'

'It was part of a longer investigation conducted by one of my top reporters. Mind you, the only spectacular thing about it is that R?dulescu, former and possibly future President of Romania, hid this fact from the public for so many years. There's nothing wrong with being of Roma extraction. He chose to make a secret of it, but I believe the public is entitled to know exactly who the politicians they are voting for really are.'

'And you don't believe that publishing this material at this precise moment in time, with all of this fighting going on between Romanians and Romas, you honestly can't conceive that this will ruin his political career?'

'If he had mentioned this fact when he first became President of Romania, then it wouldn't have mattered now, would it? But he chose to hide it.'

'In your article, you mention that his mother is living in abject poverty and doesn't even know what her son is up to, politically speaking…'

'That's right. She lives in a house with no electricity, no phone, no running water. My reporter spoke to her and apparently her son hasn't been to see her in twenty-five years. Not even her neighbours knew exactly who her son was. So what I want to say is this: the terrible thing here is not that R?dulescu has gypsy blood, but the way he has been neglecting his mother. If he can behave like that with the woman who gave birth to him, how is he going to treat a country of twenty-three million citizens? I come from a poor family. I had to look after sheep and goats when I was a little boy, my poor parents could not afford to give me a lovely childhood. That's what it was like back then. But for me – and I think for most Romanians – parents, and especially mothers, are the most precious people in our lives. How can you leave your mother completely destitute when you were once the president of this country? Whether R?dulescu's mother is Austrian or Patagonian, it doesn't matter. What matters is that he did not take care of her at all.'

'There are rumours circulating that you were handed all these compromising materials by the current government. That they even paid you to publish them.'

'No one has enough money to buy off Cornel Ardeleanu. I think my activity over the years has proved that. All I care about is to do my job as a journalist, the best job in the world. Don't come to me with your money – I am not for sale.'

'We have Commander Movilă of the Bucharest Police on the line right now. Good evening, sir, what do you think about Ardeleanu's scoop?'

'In my job, I have to remain neutral in political matters, so that's not what I am calling you about.'

'What are you calling about, if I may ask?'

'I'd just like to say that reports about yesterday's events in the department store have been grossly exaggerated. I'd like to help clarify matters a little, ahead of the official statement made by the Ministry of the Interior, which will appear tomorrow. The incident in the department store was not a conflict between Romanians and Romas, but a personal vendetta between one particular criminal gang and the security detail of that store. We have arrested Constantin Teius, aka Titi Genocide, the leader of the criminal gang. From what we can ascertain, he wanted revenge for the death of his nephew, the child who fell to his death down the stairwell when he was being chased by two security guards in that very store a couple of weeks ago. A detail worth noting: Titi Genocide is not of Roma origin, and the group he sent to attack the supermarket was composed of both Romas and Romanians. Meanwhile, the most badly wounded security guard is a Roma. So I would like to ask you report responsibly about such matters and not add to the tensions. It was a different matter in Constanța and in Movila, and we sincerely hope there won't be a repeat of those types of incidents. But what happened here in Bucharest was a simple settlement of accounts. The guilty parties will all be punished and I will keep you updated as we receive further information.'

'You see, that's what I'm afraid of,' Ardeleanu continued after the Commander had hung up. 'For the past few days or weeks, R?dulescu and Nenişor Vasile have been carving a very dangerous path for themselves, one I simply cannot understand or condone. I agree that the current government is full of incompetent people, but to play around with the fire of interethnic conflict is a fool's game. R?dulescu and Nenişor are pushing us to the edge of the precipice just as much as Theodor Varlaam is.'

'Coincidentally, we happen to have Mr Radu R?dulescu on the phone right now. Good evening, sir, what would you like to say about the documents published by Mr Ardeleanu in his paper?'

'At my age, you think you've heard and seen everything it was possible to hear and see. But you, Ardeleanu, you dirty swine, you go well beyond that! How dare you say that you are not for sale? Aren't you ashamed to lie outright? How dare you snoop around in my life, talk about my family and my parents like that? Even the worst Mafia clans or contract killers know better than to bring in family members into their quarrels... So don't you dare give me lessons about ethics!'

'You should watch your tone, Mr R?dulescu. You're not going to scare me off with your ugly words.'

'Ardeleanu, you know what I know. I can't say anything about it at the moment, but you know very well that nothing in this country remains a secret for long.'

'As I've just proved in my article. And I will continue to find out all the secrets that shouldn't really be secrets. Are there any lies in what I said? Isn't that lady your birth mother, whom you haven't seen in twenty-five years?'

'You live in a very sad world, Ardeleanu. The only mother I ever knew was the one who raised me when my father was in prison, and who died five years ago. That is the mother I loved and respected, and I gave her all the moral, legal and financial support I could. Everything else is a personal matter, something so painful and intimate, that I cannot imagine anyone wants to use them for political gain. I'm talking not only to you, but also to all the viewers who are probably befuddled by all this. Life isn't fair or beautiful. When I was just two years old, my father and I were abandoned by the woman who had given birth to me. Shortly afterwards, my father was imprisoned for his political beliefs and the woman who loved him looked after me. She is my real mother; she worked hard to offer me something resembling a normal childhood. You haven't found out all that much, Mr Ardeleanu. I loved my mother, I loved my father, and I looked after them. The rest is part of life's endless pain and misery. What you've done is inexcusable and dirty. You are a despicable creature.'

40

The podium had been set up in the corner of the reception room, and it was from its microphone that the chief of staff announced in his carefully modulated tones: 'Ladies and gentlemen, I give you: the President of Romania.'

The President entered the room accompanied by two young men dressed in snappy navy blue uniforms and approached the podium with carefully measured steps. He set his papers on it, took off his glasses and put on his reading glasses, then smiled at the audience. Warm, yet presidential. All the better-known TV channels had their cameras fixed on him, broadcasting this press conference live.

'My fellow countrymen, honoured guests, there are only a few days left until we in the Christian world celebrate the birth of Jesus Christ. Just a couple of days before that, here in Romania we commemorate the victims of the December revolution, which gave us the freedom to light our Christian candles after so many years of darkness, and allowed us to celebrate this religious event. The people who went out on the streets in December 1989, those who died there, altogether more than fifteen hundred people, most of them young people, they asked for the tyrant to leave… and he left. They asked for the fall of Communism… and it fell. They asked for freedom, and whatever you might think about the problems Romania faces nowadays, you cannot deny that we are a free country and that our people are free. They asked for food and the shops are now full of food. They asked for democracy and we now have free elections every four years and changes in government.

'What they couldn't have foreseen at that time, what none of us knew, was that all of these victories come hand in hand with harsh realities, that there is a price to pay for all of this. The shops are indeed full of food, but most Romanians lack money to purchase it. We have a free market economy – or at least we're heading in that direction – but for many of us that means unemployment, inflation, competition. It is true that we are free to say what we want, to gather in public and demand our rights, free to travel and even leave this country forever, but this freedom has also brought an increase in crime, corruption and libel perpetuated by the newspapers. Too much freedom can kill freedom, as Balzac put it. Let me be perfectly clear. We have no desire to curtail any of our hard-won liberties. But I ask you to use that freedom wisely, to exercise self-control, to have a sense of civic responsibility. No Romanian government should ever censor any of the freedoms for which we have fought so hard and with such sacrifice, but the citizens of Romania themselves can avoid its excesses.

SWORD

'For several months now someone has taken up a sword to dispense what he believes to be justice. To put things right in a world he believes to be unfair. A few days ago someone else urged all Romanians to take up their swords, forgetting the wise words of the man whose birth we will be celebrating in a matter of days. "He who lives by the sword, will die by the sword." I am not naïve, I know full well why certain political leaders advocate the use of the sword. But I ask you: if you raise the sword, will that political leader be there beside you in the ensuing disaster? Will he be the one paying the price? Not at all. He will be hiding behind his bodyguards and will leave you to bear the consequences of presenting yourselves to the rest of the world as something you are not. We Romanians, we are not assassins, we are not an intolerant nation who invades and exterminates its neighbours.

'We haven't had interethnic conflicts in Romania, even when certain people were deliberately trying to provoke them. I know we cannot boast that we have the financial acumen of the Swiss, the precision of the Germans or the determination of the Japanese. Maybe in future we will be able to develop those traits. But in the meantime, let's remain as tolerant as the Romanians. That would be the most patriotic thing we can do now.'

The President changed his glasses again and took a sip of water. His chief of staff announced that the President would now take questions for the next fifteen minutes.

'Mr President, there seems to be a personal vendetta going on between yourself and the editor-in-chief of my newspaper, Marius Ionescu. Is this why he wasn't allowed to attend this press conference?'

'There is no conflict or vendetta between me and any journalist, in this country or abroad. There are journalists who are dishonest with their readers – not just about me, but about the country in general. But that's just my personal opinion. Anyway, I'm not responsible for the list of attendees, and I actually regret that Mr Ionescu is not present. Even though my opinions may not coincide with his, I cannot deny that he holds a certain sway over public opinion in Romania. But I will tell you this much: if he had been present today, he would almost certainly not have asked the question you just asked, which proves that you are perhaps not quite at the top of your profession. There are five major TV stations filming, it's peak time for audience figures, the clock is ticking, and all you can think to ask is why your boss isn't here?'

'Sir… in your statement, you referred to the inflammatory rhetoric of Theodor Varlaam. In addition to lambasting him, are you going to take any concrete actions against the leader of the National Unity Movement?'

'The separation of powers in the state expressly forbids me from doing that. I have asked the prosecution office to run an inquiry into this matter, to see if what he has done can be described as illegal. But all of the legal procedures are pointless if people follow the call to action of this man. That's why I felt I had to intervene and appeal for calm.'

'Is the legal system moving too slowly in this case?'

'The legal system always moves slowly in a true democracy. Young, fragile democracies such as ours are always facing anti-democratic temptations. That's why I tried to address all the citizens of our country directly, regardless of what the judiciary decides. I haven't accused anyone of committing anything illegal. No matter what my personal sentiment may be, I have to uphold the law.'

'Mr President, are Romania's international relations being adversely affected by all this? There is a rumour that the German Chancellor has cancelled her visit to the OSCE Summit because of the situation here.'

'I spoke to the Chancellor two hours ago and she confirmed she would be attending the summit, albeit very briefly. She had other reasons for cutting short her visit to Bucharest. Of course the eyes of the world will be upon us on this occasion, but I have spoken personally with several of the prime ministers and presidents of EU countries and beyond, who have assured me of their full support and cooperation.'

The chief of staff said they had time for one final question.

'Would you like to comment on the recently published revelations about the birth mother of your main political rival Radu R?dulescu?'

'I have no comment to make. Mr R?dulescu is a Romanian citizen, a former president, and, while I have seldom agreed with his views, I don't believe he has ever behaved in an unpatriotic way. I don't know if that disclosure is real, and I don't care. Publishing such materials is a flagrant intrusion into someone's personal life, and I stand by Mr R?dulescu at this difficult time.'

'Mr R?dulescu suggested that the current government may have provided the materials for the newspaper to publish?'

'By no means. I can understand his anger, but let it be known that I will never tolerate bringing family matters into political arguments. I would expect the same treatment for myself. Thank you.'

41

'Good evening, dear friends. As you probably already know, the President held a short press conference at Cotroceni Palace a couple of hours ago, addressing the interethnic tensions between the Roma minority and the Romanian majority population. Mr Varlaam, although he never mentioned your name, a significant part of his speech referred to yourself as the leader of the National Unity Movement. I've invited you here because we believe in freedom of expression and in balanced reporting. How does it feel to become the main topic of a presidential declaration?'

'Good evening, Mr Preda. Congratulations on being brave enough to invite me on your show. An hour ago there was a talk show on national TV and the guests talked about me almost the entire time. I tried to call in to give my side of the story, but was not allowed on air. I then drove to the TV station but was told by a visibly embarrassed security officer: "We can't let you in, they'd go crazy merely at the mention of your name." What has the world come to when a person like me, a senator, party leader, a writer and cultural asset, is no longer allowed inside the national

TV station, because a band of opportunists have seized power and do whatever they please? I bet if I had been Hungarian, the Director General would have personally welcomed me onto the programme and arranged for subtitles to translate what I had to say. But because I am a Romanian citizen in Romania, I am sent away like a mangy dog. Luckily, there are still a handful of courageous people such as you left in the country, and that gives me hope that freedom of speech is not yet dead. Our great revolutionary thinker Nicolae B?lcescu said that nothing new can come into the world without sacrifice and pain. This is precisely what we are going through at the moment, assisting at the birth of a new Romania.'

'I asked you what you thought about the President's speech.'

'I have to admit that the President occasionally has his better moments. He wasn't bad at all tonight. Of course, the speech wasn't written by him, anyone can see that. I'm the only politician in Romania who writes his own speeches. I bet it was written by that little Jewish fellow that you had a quarrel with last week, Marinescu. He writes the speeches and his wife proofreads them. Because our poor President is an engineer, he hasn't yet fully mastered the Romanian language or history. I've spoken to him on occasion and he really struggles to string two sentences together. He's the perfect puppet for others, abroad or in the Palace. But he wasn't at all bad tonight; he'd learnt his speech by heart and recited it convincingly. I would even go so far as to say that I agree with him in principle.

'However, the President is out of touch with reality. He hasn't left the Palace unaccompanied for the past three years, because he's afraid he'll be pelted with eggs and tomatoes. He hasn't quite cottoned on yet that people are fed up. Lenin used to say "When the elites can carry on as they always have done, and when the common people no longer want to carry on as they always have done, that's when the revolution flares up." The elites have been stealing and selling off this country to all and sundry, and the common people have had enough. I travel all over the country and talk to people, really listen to them. I've seen elderly people who haven't been able to afford any meat in over a year. In the former mining towns, I've seen so much poverty, so much sadness, people without any hope, raising children without any future. The President has sent the prosecutors after me, because I have the courage to be open about the suffering. But what is he going to do when the people revolt? Shoot them? Not even Ceaușescu dared to do that, and he was a strong character, not a sock puppet. Do you think the army will be on the side of Cotroceni or that weakling who is currently serving as Defence Minister? They can shut me up, but how will they shut up millions of people? Wake up, Mr President. It's not Theodor Varlaam who is your problem, but the fact that you've brought this country to the brink of bankruptcy and national suicide. If you have any patriotism left in you, it is time to step down and call for early elections. And as the real opinion polls show, not those commissioned by the current government, the National Unity Movement will win and give this country back her dignity. You need not fear our party – by resigning, you'd demonstrate that you are a good Romanian and we would never harm a good Romanian. You've proven yourself to be incompetent, but you can still avoid becoming a traitor...'

'Mr Varlaam, can I just stop you there? A few days ago you said that you are granting honorary party membership to the serial killer nicknamed Sword. Regardless of your political beliefs, don't you think that is a risky manoeuvre?'

'Real politics relies on risk taking. It would have been so easy for me to be a two-bit politician, wandering over to Parliament whenever I feel like it, going for a drink afterwards with my colleagues, traipsing about foreign countries, and then making sure I get re-elected. I know very well that I am risking a lot with all that I have to say. I know exactly how many people are against me in this country – and who they are. But I have an eye for those who are the real enemies of this country. Yes, the man with the sword is a criminal. And he deserves to be condemned. But we can't just talk about his crimes and forget about the reasons behind his crimes. When you feel you cannot rely upon the justice system... Wasn't Vlad Țepeș a criminal in this sense? Or other great leaders? The President quoted the words of Jesus earlier: "He who lives by the sword, will die by the sword." Let me reply to that with another quote from the Bible: "God, how much longer are you going to let your people suffer?"

'No matter what people think of me, you cannot deny that I am a true patriot. I want to be judged by others who are as patriotic and committed as I am. It's all too easy to sit on the fence and not get involved, to make clever side comments instead of really caring about this country and its people. I bet there are plenty of people in the government now who are snitching on me, saying I want to make a serial killer an honorary party member. If they'd read our party manifesto clearly, they would have realised that is impossible. It's not up to me to confer party membership, it needs to be voted on by the party members. As a cultured man, an author, I tend to use metaphors, hyperbole, in my discourse. Get used to it.'

'Don't you think there is a real risk of interethnic warfare between Romanians and Romas?'

'Not a chance in hell! Come on, these are old wives' tales that they use to scare us. Because they can then declare a state of emergency, stop the independent media outlets and start arresting people. Can't you see what their scenario is? But I'm telling them now: stay in your lane, faff around a bit and pretend to be in power, sit quietly for another ten months or so until the next elections and stop messing around with things that you don't understand. After the elections we will be the winners, Varlaam and the NUM, and you will see then how real men do real politics. As for interethnic conflict, it's more likely to happen with the Hungarians, because they have Hungary to back them up and a very vocal lobbying group, as well as a strong sense of vocation due to their history. I'm a sociologist and I don't mess around with things like that. But gypsies? Let's face it, they don't really exist as a nation. The well-behaved gypsies, who mind their own business and stay away from crime, are practically Romanians. They can be MPs, ministers, anything – they just happen to be a little darker in skin tone. Romanians, real Romanians don't have a dark skin – they are fair-skinned. If you see a Romanian with a greenish kind of hue, dark lips and heavily tanned, you can bet he is either a gypsy or has a gypsy parent. But that doesn't matter as long as they behave themselves.

'But then there are the other type. What can I say about those who spread all over Europe like vermin, telling everyone they are from Romania, those who rob old ladies in the trolleybus… Let me tell you about a case which nearly broke my heart. In a bus stop in the Drumul Taberei neighbourhood, there was a little old lady, seventy years old, poor thing… Her clothes were clean, though terribly worn out. She was crying, sobbing fit to break your heart. She had just picked up her pension and her widow's allowance and they'd stolen all her money on the trolleybus. Two witnesses were there and they said that it was a band of gypsies who frequently picks pockets on this particular line, and that Bucharest Transport must surely know who they were. So there the poor old woman was, crying her heart out, and the policeman asked her to describe the pickpockets. She tried to say that she hadn't really seen them properly and he started to get nasty. Why was she wasting his time, he wasn't going to hang around all day until she remembered something, and if she wanted her money back, she had to do better than that. I went up to him – and suddenly he was all bowing and scraping: "Hello, sir, I voted for you, sir!" I gave the little old lady some money and told the policeman off for his snappy tone, but there are so many cases like it.

'Don't be surprised that Sword has supporters. Still, we're a very long way away from interethnic warfare. I learnt one thing in my childhood, that gypsies are cowards. They only attack those weaker than themselves. So nothing untoward will happen. But bear in mind that Sword would not have come to the fore if the state had been doing its job properly, if citizens could rely on the police force to protect them and on the judiciary to dispense justice. The Romanian people are very patient. In their entire history, they have only revolted a few times, but those few times have been bloody and painful. That is the lesson from history that we'd do well to remember.'

42

The President was exhausted. He lay prone on a sofa, nibbling on a chocolate biscuit. Stoicescu, Head of the Intelligence Services, and the national security adviser were in the room with him.

'It's all gone to hell in a handcart... All the effort I put into my speech and it was destroyed instantly by Varlaam. Who, incidentally, gets to talk for two hours, while I am given just twenty minutes. I don't understand – what is their game, that TV channel? And why can't we stop them? What the hell? We've been in power for three years and they just do what they damn well please... When are we going to learn to stand firm? When we lose the elections? Have you spoken to Vasilescu, the owner of the TV channel?'

'Yes, and he has guaranteed his unswerving loyalty and devotion when it comes to the elections,' his security adviser answered, 'But he asked you to help him with that nitrate factory.'

'And I gave him everything he asked for. Export licences in I don't know how many counties. He asked for an ambassadorial post for a friend of his, I gave him that. He asked to accompany me on trips abroad as one of Romania's foremost businessmen, I let him do that. He asked me to block the delivery of petrol to one of his prime rivals, and I arranged that. He wanted a part of the spoils when we privatised the cement industry, and he got more than his fair share. How does he reward me for all of this? By putting Varlaam on and taking the spotlight off me! Did you call him this evening?'

'I tried. He is travelling abroad and said he wasn't aware of any of this. He will check when he gets back.'

'Rubbish! There's nothing to check! Too late now! I told him to get rid of Preda and put Mircică in his place ... but he said that Preda is a safe bet and that he personally gets to approve everything that goes on air. What a liar!'

Stoicescu had been smoking his cigarette right next to the half-opened window, because the President did not like the smell of tobacco in his office. He now approached the President.

'Vasilescu is a rich bastard. How could he possibly be on your side? He was one of R?dulescu's old friends, there's rumours he'll be on the party list next year. So let's call a spade a spade. We are in free fall, while R?dulescu's star is rising. We'll keep on receiving this kind of criticism from now on. Remember that before the previous elections, we had few supporters. They all joined us when they saw we'd won. The rats are abandoning the ship now. But the problem isn't Vasilescu. The thorn in your side is Varlaam. I've got strong indications that he is rising in the polls. Both R?dulescu and us are losing votes to him. I've spoken to the prosecutors' office, and we could start a legal procedure against him. Vasilescu is an opportunistic toe-rag, but Varlaam is a national menace.'

'Do you have any new opinion poll figures?'

'I have sufficient proof that Varlaam's ratings are getting higher. Not just because of this crazy gypsy situation, but also because of the economic crisis, unemployment, utility bills going up and so on. Besides, his party really does have grassroots organisations in every county, unlike most of the others. He's also infiltrated all of the state institutions. I've found ten of his supporters in my own department. Turns out that up to about eight months ago they were leaking all of our documents to him. He saw exactly the same things that I saw. I told you at the time, and we resolved it quickly. But now, I think the time has come to take more serious action.'

'Don't we risk making a martyr out of him?'

'I don't care about that, Mr President. All I want is to get him out of the running for next year's elections! If no-one gets to hear from him for six months or so, his campaign is dead in the water. Varlaam is dangerous when he opens his mouth. All the other politicians agree with you when it comes to the Sword situation and interethnic conflict. Varlaam is the one who begs to differ, which makes him interesting in the eyes of the electorate. Besides, if we stop him, we will repair our image abroad. Nobody there loves him.'

'But fifteen per cent of Romanians do. Yes, I suppose it's the only path we can take right now. Any updates on Sword?'

'I believe the criminal investigators have a few leads, but nothing spectacular,' the security adviser hastened to reply, eager to shift the conversation away from Vasilescu. 'The Minister of Justice called to suggest that we move the trial of the dead policeman's brothers away from Buz?u. As you know, the village where it all happened is close to Buz?u, and they fear further violent clashes.'

'OK, I'll have a think about that. But I still don't understand why Vasilescu would give Varlaam the air time. What can that guy offer him? Vasilescu needs a peaceful country for his business, one with good relations with Europe. He's a rational businessman, after all. Does he honestly believe that he will thrive when Varlaam comes to power, if he implements even half of the idiocies he's promising?'

'The problem is that no-one takes Varlaam seriously. Nobody expects him to do anything more than shoot his mouth off. When in fact he and his party are quite ready to take control if they get elected.'

'It was all going so well.' the President interrupted himself and got up from the sofa. He'd run out of tea and biscuits. He called his chief of staff, asked for more. Then he lay down again.

'It was all going so well. The speech was short, resolute and to the point. The journalists received it very well. Did you see Ionescu apologising? We had many positive comments afterwards, from both journalists and politicians. The Minister of External Affairs called to tell me that he'd heard positive feedback from several foreign ambassadors. And now the whole painful edifice has tumbled down thanks to Preda's talk show... Oh, another thing, I want Marinescu sent away somewhere.'

'Somewhere?'

'Yes, the National Audiovisual Council or an embassy somewhere. He shouldn't be here.'

'But isn't he your speech writer?'

'He merely edits, I'm the one giving him the ideas. It's just that Varlaam said that the speech wasn't mine, and I don't want this rumour to spread. That I am incapable of writing my own speeches.'

'But no president in the world writes his own speeches.'

'I know that, but I would prefer to have him removed from the public eye. A quiet embassy post somewhere, and we can use him when we need to. Or a well-paid job in the private sector in Romania. Find something for him and we'll move him in the new year.'

The security adviser made a note in his pocket diary and got up to leave. It was two in the morning and in less than six hours he had a meeting with several generals. After he left the room, the intelligence officer pulled up his armchair closer to the President's sofa and lit his cigarette, something that only he was allowed to do and only when he was alone with the President.

'Sir, I'm afraid we may be on the brink of something that is spinning out of our control.'

'What do you mean?'

SWORD

'Tomorrow noon – or rather, today – you will receive a report, something we've been working on for several days. It's a very tense situation and if there are any new developments in the whole gypsy story, we could be in explosive territory. There have been reports of lots of minor incidents between Romanians and gypsies reported from all over the country. Nothing major, no victims. Merely a general state of wariness and anxiety. I've spoken to two sociologists about this, and they were of the opinion that, while the gypsies have never been much loved by the Romanians, they were never considered a major threat. Their criminal activities tend to be very localised and limited in scope. With the recent escalation of conflict and the way it has been politicised, the perception now is that gypsies have become a serious threat. You know that a few years back, R?dulescu and his team were circulating scare stories about the potential loss of Transylvania, and that suddenly the opinion polls showed that people were worried about interethnic conflict with the Hungarians and Transylvania being ceded to Hungary. Things they'd never seriously thought about before. When that kind of scaremongering stopped, people stopped worrying about it. We are now facing a similar situation. I believe your speech tonight was unanimously appreciated by the political classes and the media. But I fear any straw that could break the camel's back, if that Sword creature acts again…'

The President got up and started pacing. He really disliked the smell of tobacco but didn't like asking his adviser to put out his cigarette.

'So what's the plan?'

'I think you should consider a major political gesture. Something to stop all future escalation of conflict, something to prevent it.'

'Well, I asked for reconciliation this evening.'

'More than that. I think you should consider forming a government of national unity, to include all parties minus Varlaam's. And this new government should act very decisively against Varlaam.'

'Yes, I was thinking along those lines. But would it not be a bit too soon to do that?'

'I'll be honest, Mr President. I don't scare easily, but I'm asking myself if it's not too late.'

43

The cars slid noiselessly, with the headlights switched off, into the alley next to Dabuleanu's house. Captain Dulgheru of the SWAT team checked on his radio to see if the other team was in place at the back of the property. They'd had a tip-off about Dabuleanu, nicknamed Suitcase, being at home for once. There'd been a warrant out for his arrest for five years, for drug dealing and conspiracy to murder.

The captain gave the signal for his men to get out of the cars. Unfortunately, the neighbour's dog started barking hysterically, and a few other dogs joined in. They were making enough noise to wake anyone up, and sure enough, someone in the house opposite switched on the light.

Captain Dulgheru hurried to give the signal to raid the house. Two of his team members kicked in the gate and entered the front garden. The lights came on automatically and an elderly woman, half-naked, came out on the porch and started screaming when she saw the masked officers. One member of the team gently moved her aside as they entered the house. The second team had already got in through the back door and they appeared with three young men dressed in little other than their underwear, holding their hands above their heads. One of them tried to make a run for it past the police, but got the butt of a pistol in his face for his efforts and fell to the floor. In the front room there were two women with a toddler, all of them shouting at the top of their voices, swearing in both Romanian and Romani.

Dulgheru received a message on the radio that the house was all clear, but that they hadn't found Suitcase. He ordered them to look more carefully and asked the two younger women about his whereabouts. They refused to answer, merely continued cursing and shouting. He threatened to take their children away from them, but they weren't listening.

Everyone in the street was awake by now, standing in front of their gates and houses, curious to see what was happening. Police were trying to keep them at a distance from the Dabuleanu house. The two SWAT teams continued searching the property and the back garden. Dulgheru joined them in the front room and carefully examined the walls and floors. His team was searching the wardrobes. He had a sudden brainwave and asked them to move the wardrobes. First one, then two, and behind the third one, there was Suitcase, hiding in a little cavity in the wall. Dulgheru had trouble keeping a straight face. Suitcase was two metres tall, weighed 150 kilos, and he was stuffed in that hole like a Christmas turkey.

Before he could get him out of there, he got an urgent message on his police radio that the SWAT team at the back of the house were under attack. He heard machine gun fire and women screaming. More gunshots. Dulgheru grabbed Suitcase and handcuffed him, all the while shouting at his team to go and rescue the others. He was left alone with Suitcase. The massive gypsy was trying to bribe him with whatever sum he liked in return for letting him escape. Dulgheru bent over him in an effort to get the giant to stand up, when he suddenly heard the floorboards creaking behind him.

He whipped round and opened fire low, where he suspected the knees would be on a potential attacker. Dabuleanu cried out and others came running into the room.

On the floor, they saw a nine-year-old child with a bullet in his stomach.

44

The room where the Bucharest Police press conference was taking place was full to the brim with journalists, photographers and cameramen. The Commander had invited the press over following the scandal provoked by the arrest of Suitcase. He entered the room, accompanied by his deputies and his head of communications.

'Ladies and gentlemen, thank you for coming here in such numbers. I want to give you the full picture from the point of view of the Bucharest Police about the events of two days ago. We had to postpone our official statement because the Ministry of the Interior had ordered an internal investigation to understand what exactly had happened that day and who was to blame for the outcomes. As you know, two days ago, several police units, including SWAT teams, raided the premises of Sandu Dabuleanu, aka Suitcase. He had been on the most wanted list for five years, for drug dealing and conspiracy to murder. One of our officers heard from a reliable source that Dabuleanu would be at his mother's house at that time, so we went there to arrest him. I might add that when we had previously tried to arrest him several years ago, he had seriously injured a police officer. This time, our police forces were fired at and attacked with other weapons by no less than eight men from Dabuleanu's personal security team. While this fighting was going on, two people lost their lives and six were wounded. The first victim was identified as Ion Turcu, aka Oli, while the other was Marin Dabuleanu, Sandu's son. Among the injured, there were two policemen and four attackers. We also arrested twelve people who are still being questioned about their involvement in all of this, including Dabuleanu himself. We would like to express our profound regrets about the death of Marin Dabuleanu, which the Internal Affairs inquiry concluded was an unfortunate accident, which occurred during an exchange of fire between the police and the aggressors. The Ministry of the Interior ruled that the police officers had acted lawfully to defend themselves and would like to categorically deny any rumours that the units used undue force or disrespected the law of the country. I would like to underline the fact that it was Dabuleanu's gang who were the first to open fire. Thank you.'

Commander Movilă put down his papers, took off his glasses and leaned back in his chair. The press officer announced that the Q&A session was now open.

'Sir, where did you get your tip-off about Dabuleanu?'

'It came from one of our trusted sources; it was independently verified before we acted upon it. As you can see, it was entirely correct.'

'Who was the officer in charge of the operation?'

'He is one of our most experienced officers. I cannot release his name, because of the special circumstances surrounding the case. But I am keen to emphasise that he and all of the other police officers involved in the operation acted perfectly lawfully and respected all due procedures.'

'Commander, there are indications that the criminal gangs allied to Dabuleanu are preparing a series of revenge attacks. Do you think that this tense situation could lead to further interethnic conflict?'

'Can I just say that there is nothing interethnic about this case. Dabuleanu was arrested for serious crimes, including drugs, murders and kidnapping. During the arrest, several armed men opened fire against the police, who were therefore entirely justified in using their weapons. Sadly, this exchange of fire led to the death of two people. That is the whole unvarnished truth of the matter. I have no information about possible revenge, but that is an additional reason why I'm not naming any of the people involved in the operation. I would also like to ask all the media outlets to refrain from digging deeper into this and trying to find an interethnic conflict slant where there is none.'

'Commander, why did you not declare in your official statement that the second victim, Marin Dabuleanu, was just nine years old? And are you absolutely sure that the person who shot him was involved in a shoot-out? Did he give a warning and shoot in the air first, as he is required to by law?'

'What are you trying to insinuate? Both the child and the other victim were shot during a sudden rapid exchange of gunfire when Dabuleanu's bodyguards attacked the forces of order. Many of our police officers were wounded. What would you have liked them to do? Wait to be slaughtered by eight violent men with weapons? Not one of my officers wanted to cause any fatalities. But surely the responsibility lies in great part with those who resisted arrest and launched an attack against the police. The way you are approaching this is wrong. We did not shoot at a child. He was an innocent victim in an incredibly tense and dangerous situation. There's no time to give warnings and fire into the air when you are under attack by eight armed men shooting directly at you. The SWAT team had to respond instantly and they were on an official mission. Let's face it… if Dabuleanu had not been a serious drug dealer and murderer, this wouldn't have happened. Or if he hadn't been on the run from the law for five years. If they hadn't opened fire against us, if Dabuleanu had not resisted arrest, none of this would have happened. How can you blame the police for what happened instead of the drug dealers, the professional killers, the bodyguards who use illegal weapons such as machine guns? Yes, we are very sorry that a child died there. But the person who should have protected him was his father. Instead, he endangered him, putting him on the front line.'

'Dabuleanu has declared that the officer was not under fire when he shot at his son. That it wasn't a stray bullet that hit him, but he was a deliberate target.'

'I'll stop you right there. Do you realise what you are saying? You are saying that a police officer shot a nine-year-old child in cold blood, based on a dubious claim made by his father, a gang leader who sells drugs to kids of that age every day? And you refuse to believe the results of an independent inquiry that established that the police did not act unlawfully? No, you prefer to believe the criminal who is trying to find a way of getting away with a lighter sentence. Of course he wants to influence public opinion, to turn himself into a victim of police violence. Of course he does, I completely understand that. What I can't understand is why you believe him? I've been doing this job for thirty years and in all that time I've never come across a police officer who would shoot a child in cold blood. That would be a madman, not an officer. Any other questions?'

'Do you think this latest incident will create ripples abroad, now that more and more press agencies are reporting the rise of interethnic tensions between Romanians and Romas?'

'I repeat what I said previously. There was no interethnic aspect to this latest incident. Dabuleanu was a criminal and we arrested him just as we would have done with any other criminal, regardless of his ethnicity.'

'Well, there's the crux of the matter, Commander. You haven't arrested the most wanted criminal of them all, Sword. And that's why you've lost all credibility.'

45

The Minister of the Interior's special adviser walked into the coffee shop with floor-to-ceiling bay windows through which you could observe the entire street outside. The smoke inside was so thick you could cut it with a knife. The person he was supposed to be meeting was sitting at a small table, surrounded by four men all in identical black leather jackets. He was talking to a lively blonde woman, who seemed rather sparsely dressed for the cold outside.

A surveillance car was parked opposite the coffee shop. When the adviser saw it, he was tempted to turn back, but it was too late. He'd been seen entering the place, and nobody would believe he was there solely to eat chocolate chip cookies.

He walked up to the tiny table. One of the men in black stood up and motioned to him to sit in his place, while their boss was finishing his conversation with the blonde woman. The four of them had been busy discussing various developments in Romanian football, while the blonde was trying to convince her conversation partner of the sincerity of her sentiments.

A sullen waitress brought tea and two plates full of cookies. The four men switched to discussing their sex lives. One of them had had a relationship with a waitress and was sharing details of their intimate moments with the others. The blonde burst into tears when she saw that she was failing to convince her partner and left the table in a huff. The man raised his eyebrows at the ministerial adviser and gestured that he should come closer, to sit in the chair recently vacated by the young lady.

'My name is Vlad,' the adviser introduced himself and shook the man's hand.

'I am Lucan,' the man was extremely soft spoken, almost whispering. 'Drink?'

'I've got a tea, thank you.'

One of the many mobile phones on the table rang. Lucan answered, still in the same whispering tone, barely audible. After he finished his phone conversation, he lit a cigar and leant back, inhaling deeply, looking out the window. Vlad waited. After about three minutes of smoking, Lucan turned to him.

'Tell your boss that in a couple of days there will be a big demonstration in front of the government building.'

'Demonstration?'

'A few thousand gypsies are planning to protest against the death of that child. At the same time, Varlaam has been persuaded to bring some of his people out to protest. Because he's heard that the President is planning to get your boss to punish the officer who shot the lad. Captain Dulgheru.'

It was on the tip of Vlad's tongue to ask how he knew the name of the officer, but he stopped himself in time.

'The President is under pressure from human rights activists and EU ambassadors, that's why he wants Dulgheru to stand trial. Varlaam is coming out with his clique to protest against that. Tomorrow Cornel Ardeleanu's newspaper will start a campaign against Dulgheru. They'll even plaster his picture on the front page. So, if those two hostile groups meet in front of the government building, you can imagine all hell will break loose. And the only person who has anything to gain out of it all is R?dulescu, because he's keeping his hands clean.'

'Why is Ardeleanu getting involved?'

'Well, the President has him by the short and curlies with some recordings, while R?dulescu has bought him for a handsome sum. So, he's somewhere in the middle and trying to negotiate with both of them. Tell your boss that a major cabinet reshuffle is in the pipeline and his job is up for grabs. It will likely go to either Constantinescu or Nemeș.'

Vlad was taking notes. He asked Lucan if he had any idea how to avoid the confrontation between the demonstrators in front of the government building.

'Of course. Get your boss to make a public announcement, on national TV, that he is banning all demonstrations.'

'He can't forbid them!'

'Well, then he should be creative about it. He has to stay a step ahead of them, to box them in. And tell him to stop defending Dulgheru so much.'

'I don't think he'll listen to me about that. You know how defensive he gets when any of his men are attacked.'

'He shouldn't defend him if he isn't sure what he's defending. Dulgheru did shoot that child while he wasn't under attack. He heard a noise, got scared and killed him. All the police reports are false and it will all come out in the end.'

'What are you saying?'

'Dulgheru shot that child even though no-one was shooting at him at the time. The boy was in that room with his father, Suitcase. When Suitcase hid behind the wardrobe, the boy hid as well. Maybe he thought it was a game. Anyway, he came out when he saw that his father had been found and handcuffed. When the little squirt came out, Dulgheru got a fright, because he thought the two adults were the only ones in the room, so he shot him. Yes, there was gunfire outside, but not in that room. Do you get it? And the police, Commander Movil?, all the others are covering that up, declaring that it all happened in an exchange of fire. So tell your boss to shut up and stop defending them. He should say he'll investigate matters further. Dulgheru won't wriggle out of it, that's for sure.'

46

The OSCE Summit in Bucharest has finished. We had presidents, prime ministers and ministers joining us here in our capital city. They discussed all sorts of important issues and no doubt made many important decisions. What's more: it all went smoothly. Of course, there were a few minor niggles. The microphone cut out just as the American Secretary of State was giving his speech. The wife of the Czech foreign secretary was not allowed into her villa on the first day. The food tasted weird and two of the official limos crashed into each other just outside the Palace of the Parliament. But all's well that ends well. The official pictures show all of the participants smiling, the official statements were all quite positive, and, above all, nobody mentioned the elephant in the room: interethnic conflict. Luckily, Sword has not been active these past few weeks, the Romas did not demonstrate in front of the Parliament as expected, and even Varlaam didn't make any incendiary remarks.

In a couple of days it will be December 21st – it feels like such a long time ago already that we've nearly forgotten what happened on that day. And then we have the festive season approaching, Christmas, New Year, *all the saints' days – Ștefan, Vasile and Ion. Practically half the population of Romania will be celebrating their name day ... and while we are off celebrating, the government has to decide how to solve this problem.*

Thus far we've had a relatively balanced situation. It's precarious, but balanced. But now we risk tipping over into something far more serious with this Dabuleanu affair. It is scandalous for the government. Yes, Dabuleanu was a criminal, he deserved to get caught and to pay for his crimes. But his son is not to blame for the fact that his father was a gangster. Yet the police shot him like a criminal. At first they tried to present his death as an unfortunate accident during a rapid exchange of gunfire. Other sources, however, claim that the events implicate a senior officer. At the very least, he could be accused of negligence, if not more.

One of our major newspapers published a dossier about the Dabuleanu affair yesterday, accusing Captain Dulgheru of cold-blooded murder and Commander Movil? of attempting to cover that up. Simple, you might say, let's punish them for misleading the public! Alas, it's not that simple! An opinion poll shows that more than seventy per cent of the population support Dulgheru and consider that he was simply doing his duty. Our newspaper is not the only one that has been bombarded with letters from the public written in support of Dulgheru.

Our sources at Cotroceni Palace say that the President is being pressurised by international human rights organisations who have turned up in Bucharest to demand that the policeman be punished. The international press has this case under intense scrutiny.

SWORD

Here's the dilemma, which to prioritise – internal or external image? The current government has always been keen to maintain its reputation abroad. But it can't afford to do that now, when there are only ten months to go until the next election. One false step and their campaign goes down the drain. One more problem is that punishing the policeman will lead to a breakdown in trust between the President and the Ministry of the Interior, which is closer to Theodor Varlaam. So what next, Mr President? The ball is in your court and I doubt you will have a restful Christmas holiday in your palace in Cotroceni. It might well be your last Christmas there.

Speechwriter Marinescu and the presidential security adviser were face to face with their boss, who was looking accusingly from one to the other.

'There you go – Adrian Maier is attacking me too now! What's he after? You told me to get rid of my spokesman, because his relationship with the media wasn't all that great. I kicked him out. Then you said my communications advisor was rubbish, so I got rid of him, although that put me on bad terms with his mother. I mean, he really was crap, but still... What more do I need to do for it to work?'

'Mr President, no-one can keep the press in check,' Marinescu dared to speak up, 'Especially not in the fourth year in power and when you are lagging ten percentage points behind the other candidate. If it will make you feel better, I can resign here and now. And I don't need a job with the National Audiovisual Council, nor an ambassadorial post somewhere. But anyone who tells you that they can control the media is lying.'

'But when I hired you, you said you'd be able to keep the press in check.'

'Yes, if I've got ammunition of the type we had for Cornel Ardeleanu. If I've got contracts with which to bribe the papers or TV channels, like we do with Mircică and with Rusu. But Maier.... We've never given him anything and we can't threaten him with anything. Besides, the article is not really offensive, is it? It's slightly dangerous because of certain things we know, but it's not as if he's attacking you personally.'

'What do you mean? He says quite clearly that it will be my last Christmas here.'

'Let's face it, Mr President. At the risk of spoiling your evening, most of the members of your team believe the same thing.'

'Including you?'

'Yes. I have to admit I think it will be extremely difficult to win the elections next year. But maybe I am too pessimistic.'

'So why don't you abandon me then?'

'Pessimism is one thing, loyalty is another.'

The President fell silent, then gave Marinescu a sly smile. He'd already decided to get rid of the man, now he'd been given a proper justification for removing him.

'OK, what's happening at Interior?'

The security adviser opened up his notebook and began to read out loud, slowly and mechanically, as if he were a robot.

'The internal inquiry regarding Dulgheru is proceeding rapidly and will find him at fault. He will then be sent to face the courts. Once it is proven that Movil? misled the judiciary, he will be forced to retire, as will the other eight officers who took part in the cover-up. We are not sure yet what will happen to the Minister. He never pronounced himself clearly on this case, always avoided getting entangled in the affair. We know he met Dulgheru twice away from his office.'

'And what are the consequences if we sentence Dulgheru?'

'Bad, no matter how you look at it.'

'Isn't it strange? Dulgheru killed the boy through negligence and nobody really cares, because he is the son of a gypsy gangster. Maybe Maier is right after all? If I sentence Dulgheru, I will almost certainly not get re-elected in autumn. But if I don't sentence him, then every door in Europe will slam shut in my face.'

47

The Christmas decorations were up on the two main boulevards in the centre of Bucharest. The city was bathed in an orange glow. It was snowing, but that didn't deter the crowds in the shops and on the streets. It was nearly Christmas, after all. You could tell that simply by looking at the little groups of child buskers, some dirtier than others, who were trying to squeeze money out of the passers-by with their strikingly unusual renditions of Christmas carols.

Melania Dulgheru had finished nearly all her shopping. Her arms were aching from the heavy bags, despite the fact that she also had two policemen accompanying her. When her husband's name had been splashed all over the front pages, her boss had arranged for two officers to see her home after work every evening. She knew it was taking goodwill a bit too far to have the two men go shopping with her, but it was Christmas after all. She had been working in the Ministry of the Interior for fifteen years and had never felt the need for extra protection. Since the launch of the media campaign against her husband, she'd started receiving messages of support and solidarity from the most unexpected sources. The Minister himself had called her into his office, assured her that her husband had his full support, but that he was being pressured from above into punishing Dulgheru. Her husband had been under so much stress lately that she'd decided to make even more of an effort to get him some nice presents, buy things to cook a lovely Christmas meal and, with the children shipped off to the grandparents in Sibiu, maybe they could have a romantic evening together.

The two officers helped her into the car and drove her home. She had bought a bottle of wine for each of them, as a sort of thank you present. At first they were shy about accepting it, but she insisted. The mood brightened considerably. When she got out of the car, they told her that they were sure there was no cause for concern, that Captain Dulgheru had merely been doing his job and obeying orders.

The staircase was dark and she regretted not asking one of the men to accompany her all the way to the lift. But then she saw her ground-floor neighbour taking out his bin and he switched on the light for her. In the lift, she told herself that if the police kicked her husband off the force, it was their loss, not his. He'd already received several attractive offers from private security firms. Yes, there was a bit of an uproar in the media right now, but it would die down eventually.

When she got to her floor, she put down the heavy bags outside the door and knocked three times. The code established with her husband. He never rang the bell, but knocked a certain number of times to let her know that it was him. No reply. She knocked again but couldn't hear any sound coming from their flat. She tried to peek through the peephole but could see no light. Maybe he'd taken an afternoon nap, now that he was confined to the house all day.

She took out her keys and unlocked the door. She carried her bags to the kitchen and started to unpack. She put the wine and the food in the fridge, and hid the Christmas presents behind the barrel of pickled cabbage in the pantry. She went through to the bedroom without switching on the light. Her husband was lying on his back on the bed, a damp patch next to his head. He held a pistol in one hand and a white piece of paper in the other.

48

It is difficult to write about the violent death of a person. Sadly, in the last few months, we have had far too many cases where we had to do just that. We have had people with their throats cut by a serial killer, we've had young men burnt alive while doing their duty, we've had villagers beaten to death because of intolerance, children who were in the wrong place at the wrong time, and policemen committing suicide because they can no longer cope with the media scrutiny. Our society is going through a tragic period right now and there is little of the Christmas spirit floating around.

Of course, our country is resilient. It has been through much trauma in the past one hundred years alone: the uprising of the far-right Iron Guard, American bombing, German bombing, Soviet invasion, labour and re-education camps building the Canal, an as yet heavily-contested number of deaths during the 1989 Revolution, miners destroying the capital city, clashes between ethnic Romanians and Hungarians in Târgu Mureș, arson attacks, football hooliganism and Varlaam's obscene hate speeches.

So yes, we've been through a lot. But I have to say that the present situation has all the hallmarks of fuel being added to the flames. It could lead to an explosion of such a scale that we cannot even begin to comprehend it. That is why we need to remain clear-headed and cautious, and help those around us to keep a clear head as well.

That is why I declare here, with a heavy heart and with apologies to Captain Dulgheru's family, that he was wrong to shoot the little boy and that it was only right that he should bear the consequences of that. However, he preferred to choose death rather than dishonour. Those were his final words in the suicide note found by his bedside. I have no doubt that the tragic death of this fine officer will lead to political manoeuvres and extremist reactions. I have heard that Varlaam's vultures are eager to make the deceased an honorary member of their party and to conduct a memorial service for him tomorrow, 21st December. The atmosphere within the Ministry of the Interior seems to have reached breaking point. Meanwhile, the police blame the ministry for Dulgheru's death.

I may risk alienating all my readers, but I have to admit that the state was justified in acting swiftly to order a detailed inquiry into the death of the child. The people who are really to blame in this matter are the senior police officers, especially Commander Movil?, who tried to obfuscate the truth about this case, thereby giving rise to all sorts of rumours and contradictions.

To all those of you who think that the state was wrong to ask for an official inquiry, I would like to propose a very simple test. Regardless of where you stand on the political spectrum, if that had been your child who had been shot, what would you have liked to see? Would you have wanted the state to get involved or not? Would you have liked them to organise a cover-up to protect one of their officers, or would you have wanted to be reassured that all the state institutions are functioning normally and independently, and that justice is done? Let's set aside the ethnic origin of the child or his parents' criminal background. We cannot live in a country where, at the start of this new millennium, a child is shot, whether accidentally or not, and there are no consequences as a result of that. We have to understand this principle. Of course, it does not preclude us from expressing our sorrow at the personal tragedy of the Dulgheru family.

'I never thought I'd live to see the day when Marius Ionescu is not having a go at me!' The President positively beamed after he read the article. 'See, all he wanted was a little attention. I sat down to talk to him and he's come to heel now like a pet dog. They're all the same, these journalists. You have to show that you care about their opinion. Prove that you've read a couple of their articles. Let's face it – they all want my position. Who was it that said that Romania has twenty-three million potential presidents, but there is only one position available. And it's only available every four years. You can imagine how frustrating that must be for everyone else!'

Stoicescu of the Intelligence Services nodded and kept his thoughts to himself. There was no point in contradicting the President, but he was pretty sure that Ionescu had written exactly what he believed and would not hesitate to attack the President again when the occasion arose.

'What's happening with the Minister of the Interior?' asked the President, with one eye still on Ionescu's opinion piece.

'He is going to resign. Which isn't good at all.'

'Why not? Let him go! Thanks to this scandal, we managed to get rid of some senior officers we were unable to budge before. If he's the next one to resign, the Ministry becomes in essence ours. We'll appoint Constantinescu in his place and it's all done.'

'No, it isn't. Constantinescu is going to need at least six months to get up to speed. It's a volatile and complex environment at present, completely the wrong moment to lose an experienced minister. He has a certain influence with his people, he's managed to control his ministry.'

'Nonsense. He has zero influence. Nobody pays any attention to him. Besides, what would you have me do? He's the one who decided to resign. Nobody's kicking him out! Anyway, just to be on the safe side, I'd like you to get in touch with the City Hall and the Cabinet, also the Prime Minister. I want them to forbid the public gathering organised by Varlaam. Although it's tempting to let him go ahead with it and make a fool of himself. Then we would really be able to get rid of him for good!'

'No, sir, it would be best to not allow them to go ahead with the public gathering. I fear the public reaction – and besides, there will be demonstrations tomorrow by those who participated in the 1989 revolution. If those two factions meet, sparks will fly.'

49

Aurel was called Ostrich by all his friends and work mates, because he was very tall, with a small head in proportion to his body, and a rather prominent beaked nose. He'd been working as a cab driver for twenty-five years. He knew Bucharest like the back of his hand and, unlike most other drivers, he was pretty good at repairing his car as well. Shortly after the 1989 revolution he'd tried to make a go of it by starting his own business, but he nearly went bankrupt after a year or so. So he preferred to work for a company. He was given a brand-new car, and if he needed some extra income, he could occasionally repair his neighbours' cars.

He thought he'd seen everything in the course of a quarter of a century doing this job. All sorts of famous people had been in his cab, politicians, actors, footballers, writers, beautiful women... One couple had got into such an acrimonious fight in his cab that they decided then and there to get a divorce. Another time, this was on a winter night back in Ceaușescu's era, a woman had given birth in the back of his car.

But what had happened earlier this evening had marked him in a way that made it rank right up there with the worst experiences he'd ever had. A couple had got into his cab in the centre of town, at Roman? Square. The man was around sixty, well-dressed and fragrant. The woman was about twenty-five, likewise immaculately dressed. It was cold outside, their cheeks were red from the cold. But after a couple of minutes, things started to heat up. They were kissing, cuddling, pulling off their clothes. Ostrich tried to be discreet, but it was impossible to pretend that he didn't notice what was happening in the back seat. At some point, he stole a look in his rear-view mirror and caught the young lady giving him a sorrowful look, while the elderly gentleman was otherwise engaged. She did not look uncomfortable or embarrassed or indifferent. Her face was just incredibly sad… He dropped them off in front of a villa in the posh neighbourhood of B?neasa, By that point, she seemed to have recovered her cheerful spirits, and he got an excellent tip from the man. But her melancholy gaze haunted him for ages afterwards.

It was starting to rain. The rain soon turned into sleet and then snow. Through the driving flakes, he saw someone trying to hail him. He stopped the car and three youngsters got in, shivering. They wanted to go to Giuleşti, they said. Just as he was getting onto the Grant Bridge, they changed their mind and said they would rather go to Militari. They were whispering among themselves, which made Ostrich suspicious. He made sure his two-way radio system was on, so that his boss could hear him.

They got to Militari, where the boys told him to drive into some side streets. He asked for the exact address, but they couldn't come up with a name, asking him to turn right, no left, second right… they weren't sure, they were here on a visit…

Ostrich started to feel really uncomfortable and pressed the panic button. That meant that Central Despatch was aware something was wrong and would radio other drivers who were close by to check in on him and even send a security car. His boss had an arrangement with a security firm to send an emergency intervention vehicle if things got volatile. The youths in the back continued giving him contradictory information, unsure where they were heading. In his rear-view mirror, he saw first one taxi, then another one following him. He was safe.

He asked the boys where they were going and if they had enough money to pay. One of the lads told him to shut up and swore at him. Ostrich stopped the car and tried to get out, but the guy in the middle grabbed hold of him and held a knife to his throat. They told him to hand over all his money. He tried to remain calm and pretended to search his pockets.

The car doors were opened up and the youths were dragged out of the vehicle. While the one in the middle was distracted by the sight of his friends on either side of him being pulled out, Ostrich managed to grab his knife and disarm him. There were at least ten other taxis around, plus the security vehicle. The police were there too. There were about fifteen men in all, punching and kicking the three youths. Ostrich was still holding onto the guy who'd pulled a knife on him, and he too started hitting him until the blood gushed from his nose and mouth. The policemen were the most violent of all, beating them with their truncheons and swearing loudly.

That's when Ostrich remembered the story about Dulgheru. He realised that at least two of the three youths were gypsies. Suddenly, the police announced that reporters were coming. They hastily put handcuffs on the young men, stuffed them all into the same car and took them to the police station. The other taxi drivers melted away from the scene in less than three minutes. By the time the TV reporters arrived, ready to film, the only people they could find were the few onlookers who had braved the blizzard to see what was happening just outside their doors.

50

The traffic had been stopped again at University Square. There was a white banner blocking off access to the entrance to the square, the very place where the anti-government protesters had set up their first barricade back in 1989. Cars were being diverted towards Batiștei Street. It was a bright and unseasonally warm morning, all the more surprising because there'd been a bit of snowfall overnight. The sun was reflected in the windows of the Intercontinental Hotel and the sky was a perfectly transparent blue.

There they all were, gathered around the monument dedicated to the victims of 1989: state officials, a few hundred army officers, a couple of hundred revolutionaries, journalists and photographers, plus diplomatic representatives from the foreign embassies. Behind them in the square were several hundred more locals. The fine weather had tempted them out of their houses.

The Prime Minister was awaiting his turn to set down the floral wreath. His mind was running more towards the negotiating team from the World Bank, whom he was due to meet again very shortly.

He'd have skipped the ceremony if he could, but the President had insisted that he had to take part.

Two kilometres to the north of this state ceremony lay Victoria Palace, the seat of the government. At the present moment, it was surrounded by police cordons, awaiting the arrival of Varlaam's protesters. Although both the City Hall and the Ministry of the Interior had expressly forbidden any demonstrations, Varlaam had not cancelled the protest, at least not as far as anyone knew. More than a thousand people were gathered in front of the building, mostly from the counties surrounding Bucharest, but no sign of Varlaam.

Back at University Square, a priest was holding a short mass, which caught the Prime Minister by surprise. He noticed the Minister of Defence gesticulating wildly, letting him know that he still had his hat on. The PM hurriedly took it off, bowed his head and made the sign of the cross together with the other officials gathered there. The President had just laid his wreath, then it was the turn of the various associations of revolutionaries, and then finally it would be his turn. He was very annoyed about the resignation of the Minister of the Interior. The person the President wanted to appoint was lacking in any kind of experience or knowledge in that area, and, if the report from the Intelligence Services was to be believed, he was also far from being as pure as driven snow.

His mobile phone started vibrating in his pocket. He tried to take it out discreetly to see who it was, but without his glasses on he couldn't make out a thing. He couldn't talk anyway, so he switched it off and put it back in his pocket. The revolutionaries were laying down their wreaths, kneeling in front of the monument and then stepping back quietly. His aide prodded him that it was his turn. He went up to the monument, bent down to lay the wreath, made the sign of the cross and rejoined the line of state officials.

No sooner had he rejoined them, when the President whispered that there seemed to be trouble brewing at Victoria Palace. Just then, his aide came up to inform him that the protestors had broken through the police cordons and were inside the government building.

51

'Ladies and gentlemen, we are live from Victoria Palace. Our special correspondent Dan Dumitrescu is there to tell us about the latest developments from the public protest. What can you tell us, Dan?'

'As you can see, the entire square is enveloped in tear gas. I can barely breathe... Approximately one hour ago, the National Unity Movement protesters had gathered here to demonstrate against the government's decision to pursue a public inquiry into the case of Captain Dulgheru. They believe this decision led to his suicide. So, as I was saying, less than an hour ago, the protestors managed to break through the police cordon and force their way into the building. Eyewitnesses say that the whole confrontation lasted less than five minutes and that the police officers were stood down from the front of the building, leaving it entirely at the mercy of the intruders. As far as we can tell, the protesters have damaged several of the rooms, smashed windows and even set fire to some objects. A quarter of an hour ago the police and military reinforcements arrived, including SWAT teams, and they managed to chase the intruders out of the building. The number of protesters has risen from fifteen hundred this morning to around ten thousand at present. The military used tear gas to disperse the crowds. Demonstrators are now regrouping towards the entrances to the metro station. Further clashes have been reported between the NUM protesters and the former revolutionaries who came right away from University Square when they heard that the government building was under attack.'

'Are there any victims?'

'We have seen some wounded, a few quite seriously, but we have no reports of any fatalities.'

'What is happening inside the government building now?'

'It is now under the control of the police forces and firefighters who are putting out the fires started by the protesters. The whole square is under police supervision, but the demonstrators refuse to leave the area. They have retreated to the public subway on Titulescu Boulevard and behind the Natural History Museum. The revolutionaries who came to help the government forces have also been evacuated from the square.'

'And is Theodor Varlaam there with his crowd?'

'He is indeed. Apparently, he tried to stop the protesters from entering the government building and just a few minutes ago he negotiated an end to the conflict with the officer in charge.'

'Thank you, Dan. We will rejoin you in Victoria Square shortly. Meanwhile, let's go over to Cotroceni

Palace, where we have our correspondent Raluca Nistor.'

'Good afternoon, Irina. The Cabinet is holding an emergency meeting as we speak here at Cotroceni Palace. The President, the Prime Minister and all of the coalition party leaders are also present. Radu R?dulescu, the main opposition party leader, arrived just a few minutes ago. And I might add that the Minister of the Interior, who resigned yesterday, is also here.'

'What is the purpose of this meeting?'

'According to our sources, there was something unusual about the behaviour of the police forces this morning in front of Victoria Palace. Sources from the President's office claim that they abandoned their positions and thereby facilitated the storming of the building. The Ministry of the Interior claims that they were caught by surprise, that the attackers were stronger and better co-ordinated than they expected. One of the senior police officers I spoke to earlier today, who asked to remain anonymous, says that their morale and trust has been at a low ebb since the suicide of Captain Dulgheru, resulting from the official inquiry into his actions and those of eight other members of his SWAT team. We expect that following this emergency meeting at Cotroceni, there will be a cross-party condemnation of the actions of the protesters and the attack on a government building. There is even talk of lifting parliamentary immunity from Theodor Varlaam and other NUM MPs.'

'Thank you, Raluca. As you can see, dear viewers, Romania has once more fallen prey to social unrest just before the Christmas holidays. The escalation of interethnic conflict, the unresolved Sword case, the extremist nationalist declarations of Varlaam have led to this explosion of violence. It's difficult to predict what the consequences of this might be, but we have invited the well-known political analyst Sergiu Enescu into our studios to try to shed some light on the matter. So, Mr Enescu, what will happen next, do you think?'

'I just want to tell you that before coming on air, I had a short conversation with a friend of mine, a French journalist based in Brussels. I asked him how he and his peers view this Romanian problem. And I have to admit his answer calmed me down somewhat. He said that there have always been explosions of violence all over the world. There will always be extremist groups attacking the principles of law and order. If the state intervenes while adhering strictly to public law and democratic principles, then there's no issue. The demonstrators attacked the government headquarters, set fire to rooms and smashed windows. The police intervened to stop them. There's nothing more to that and I'm sure politicians in the West will agree with that.'

'Do you believe that the police whose mission it was to guard the government headquarters actually allowed Varlaam's protesters into the building?'

'Dear lady, the government was absolutely right in commissioning an official inquiry into the death of that child. It's far more likely that the police were intimidated by the fury of the protesters. We cannot afford to sanction the police yet again, or there will be no-one left on our streets to protect us. What we should do is sanction Varlaam, not deplore the lack of confidence of an eighteen-year-old police officer facing a crowd of noisy protesters.'

'Our correspondent said that Varlaam tried to prevent the demonstrators from entering the building.'

'He shouldn't have taken them there in the first place. The demonstration was illegal and he went ahead with it nevertheless. This is the moment to take firm measures against Varlaam. He has to disappear from our political life.'

52

'Good evening, everyone! Welcome to our special edition tonight, in which we attempt to analyse the events that have rocked our country over the past twenty-four hours. Yesterday, 21st December, the President, the Prime Minister and several other Cabinet members were busy laying wreaths to commemorate the anniversary of the 1989 revolution. Meanwhile, over five thousand protesters attacked and occupied the government headquarters in Victoria Palace for about half an hour. Police forces managed to clear the building of the intruders and there were multiple arrests. All the political parties (with the exception of the NUM) released a joint statement condemning these violent actions and asking for the perpetrators to be punished. The President also released a personal statement asking for cross-party collaboration and action against hate speech, extremism and intolerance. The Prosecution Service has launched an investigation against the protestors, who seem to have been largely NUM party members or sympathisers. This is, of course. the party led by Theodor Varlaam.

'Mr Varlaam was present in the square at the time but tried to stop the demonstrators from attacking the building – unsuccessfully – and then negotiated a truce between the police forces and the protesters. A parliamentary commission has been set up to examine the degree of involvement of Theodor Varlaam and other NUM MPs in the violent incidents which took place that day.

'This morning, fifteen retired generals published a harshly-worded open letter, in which they express their concern at the – I quote – *systematic abuse of our uniformed personnel*. They consider it intolerable that people in uniform, who are merely doing their duty and following orders, should be publicly mocked and trampled upon for political expediency or because someone outside this country demands it. The statement continues as follows: *It was the army who enabled the creation of a modern, post-communist nation, and the people in uniform have always protected the borders and the dignity of this country. It is shameful that our current government seeks to placate foreign governments and interests by sacrificing its officers.* As I said, this letter was signed by fifteen senior military leaders, now retired. To discuss this matter, I've invited the following guests in our studio. General Dumbrava, former head of the General Staff of the Armed Forces, Mr Romușan, state secretary at the Ministry of Defence, and the well-known journalist Marius Ionescu. Good evening, gentlemen. General, why did you sign this open letter?'

'Good evening, Mr Preda. This statement came about after a great deal of soul-searching and concern about the problems facing Romania today. There are fifteen of us who signed it, but there are hundreds more, including active senior officers, who agree with what we have laid out there. You are all aware that the Army is one of the most respected institutions in this country, on a par with the Church. Going back in history, we can see that these two institutions have often been the only elements of stability that the citizens of our country could count on, that they enabled us to survive as a nation. Yet we cannot help but notice a degradation in the working conditions of our armed forces and the increasing contempt with which they are being treated by politicians. Please note that I am not talking just about the military, but also our police forces. The recent Dulgheru case was the straw that broke the camel's back, as far as we're concerned. Yesterday's protests showed just how attached the Romanian population is to its true values. They didn't come out to demonstrate for higher salaries or pensions or food. They came out to protest because Captain Dulgheru's fate moved them. In all of this brouhaha and scandal, let's not forget the basic principle of military and police structure: you have to obey orders. If this principle does not hold true, then there is no effective army. And all that Dulgheru did was obey orders.'

'Nobody ordered him to shoot a child,' Ionescu couldn't help but intervene.

'Ah, Mr Ionescu, I read your article yesterday. And you are right, with your civilian hat on. But Dulgheru was not a civilian, so you have to judge him as a man who spent his entire life following orders. And his orders were to catch that gypsy.'

'That criminal, you mean?'

'Why should I censor my words? He was a gypsy, wasn't he? And if he hadn't been a gypsy, there wouldn't have been so much fuss about this case. If the victim had been a Romanian child, nobody would have bothered. The EU protects minority rights, they don't care about the majority. So Dulgheru was told to arrest that gypsy who was a drug dealer and also implicated in several serious crimes. He finds him holed up behind a wardrobe. He bends over to put handcuffs on him and then hears the sound of gunfire and on his radio he hears that his men were under attack. He sends his officers to investigate and is convinced that it's just him and the criminal left in the room. When he suddenly hears footsteps behind him, not from the doorway – where you might have expected his own men to appear – but from across the room, he turns and shoots – at knee level, as he's been trained to do. How could he have known that it was a child and that knee-level would be at the level of that child's abdomen? Those are the simple facts in the Dulgheru affair.'

'If the facts are so simple, then why did eight senior officers from the Ministry of the Interior, including Commander Movilă, falsify their reports?'

'Because they realised what the consequences would be and because they were trying to save their colleague. Every officer has a spirit of loyalty to his fellow officers. They are all driven by something that is sadly lacking in Romanian society nowadays: a sense of honour.'

'Excuse me, General, I may be a dishonourable civilian,' Ionescu broke in, 'Although I deeply regret what happened to Captain Dulgheru and am very sorry for his family, Romania must not become under any circumstances the kind of country where a man – however honourable he might be – can shoot whomsoever he pleases and then hide behind notions of law and order and the privileges conferred by a uniform. We are not at war, there is no national emergency and I don't think your uniform confers you more rights than my civilian clothing. You know why? Because I help to feed that uniform – yours, those with even more stars than yours, and even the simple undecorated foot soldier. I pay my taxes and my dues for people like you. I accept a lower budget for health so that your ministry has a higher budget for defence, and I am the foolish onlooker who doesn't complain when those in uniform break the law, build themselves eye-wateringly expensive villas with ill-gotten gains and laugh at my poverty and good faith. General, Romania is a civilian state. And the small, humble civilian is entitled to be protected by the army, the police, the gendarmes, the firemen. Not to be led by them.'

'Mr Ionescu, are you naïve or merely good at twisting other people's words? I don't disagree with anything that you said – or rather, I disagree with only one aspect of it. You say that Romania is not at war. You are wrong – we are at war. What's worse, in 1989 Romania lost a war. The population took to the streets and chanted some jingles, but the truth is that the military bloc we were a part of, the Warsaw Pact, was vanquished. And the victors, the ones we are so eager to curry favour with right now, still treat us like a vanquished nation. The current peace is a false one, and we are struggling to find our place within the new world order. To occupy a place comparable to what we had before 1989. Every day we face all sorts of obstacles put in our path by external forces set on undermining our national interests. And the only people standing between us and them are the people in uniform.'

The secretary of state was chomping at the bit.

'Mr Preda, might I intervene?... General, I know your background, your qualifications and I know your position on military matters. And I can only say that I honestly don't understand what you are trying to prove. We had clashes between protesters and our police forces, following the temporary occupation of the government building, there have been other clashes elsewhere in the country. Don't you think it's irresponsible to talk about a war being waged on us by occult forces from abroad? Let me be clear, Romania is not at war with anyone. Worst case scenario, we could talk about a war on poverty, but not any other kind of war!'

'Mr Romuşan, I don't know how much history you know, since you are a lawyer by training. But surely you remember that the first measure taken by the Russians in 1945 when they imposed a Communist regime upon us was to destroy our army. They arrested and executed senior officers. Of course, it's not on the same scale nowadays, but what is NATO currently doing? Imposing a reduction in numbers of our armed forces, closing down our arms industry, introducing new training methods. How many junior officers have you had to make redundant this year alone, thanks to restructuring? We are being treated like a vanquished country, sir. And yes, we might not have many other options, but we are far too willing to kneel down in front of our so-called betters from the West.'

'General, NATO is our only chance for security. Europe is our family. We would have been part of them fifty-five years ago, but for that unfortunate historical accident. How can you compare joining NATO with the Soviet occupation?'

Preda felt he had to intervene.

'General, I understand that you are also announcing the launch of a new organisation called the St George's Association. What is the purpose of this new organisation?'

'St George is the patron saint of the Romanian Army. As we know from the Bible, he was the one who killed the dragon, and the army's role is to defend the country and its people from dragons. The purpose is to be able to get involved in politics, which, as you know, the army is not allowed to do. And a good thing too, I have no issue with that. But us, we are all retired generals, no longer serving in the army, and we are joined by sociologists, political analysts and legal experts. We will be monitoring how politics intervenes in military life and generally in the life of all those who serve in uniform.'

'And what do you plan to do after you've monitored that?'

'Nothing spectacular. Merely publish our results and spark public debates about them.'

'Is that it, really?' Ionescu asked with a note of disbelief in his voice. 'Because when I heard you talk about this association, I felt a cold chill running down my spine. It reminds me a little too much of South America. Or Turkey, where every three years the army mounts another coup, shoots some disloyal journalists and then retreats once more behind the throne.'

'Well, they're not doing too badly, Turkey, are they? Used to be the poorest, most miserable country in Europe and now they are a regional leader in the Balkans and have the fifth largest army in the world.'

'But General, we are nothing like the Turks. Might I remind you that we actually fought against them for about five centuries.'

'Mr Ionescu, stop playing around with words and concepts. I know you are an honest man, but sometimes you fail to see the bigger picture. Those in power currently have diminished the army, just like our newest history manuals have diminished our history. Our children are now taught that Stephen the Great was a philanderer rather than a serious leader, that Vlad Țepeș was a madman, that Mihai the Brave was a two-bit adventurer. The truth may lie somewhere in between, but you cannot strip us entirely of our dignity. You can take away our economic independence, our political independence, our national defence. But at least leave us our legends. Sadly, the Romanian army is nothing but a legend now. All we can do is look back upon our heroic past, when we decided our own fate thanks to those brave men on the frontline.'

'General, are you sure that Romanians want a stronger role for the army? I personally doubt that.'

'Mr Ionescu, do you know how many people would like a military regime?'

'No.'

'So, Mr Romușan, are you going to tell him or shall I?'

'What is he referring to, Mr Romușan?'

'It's an in-depth study commissioned by the Ministry of Defence, but it was supposed to be only for internal consumption.'

'Well, if you don't want to talk about it, Mr Romușan, I will. I've got all the numbers right here in front of me. When the surveyed people were asked if they would like a military regime, thirty-eight per cent said no, twenty-two per cent either didn't answer or didn't know, while forty per cent said yes, they would. Of those forty per cent, when asked why they would like a military regime, eighty per cent of them replied that it would help bring order to the country.

Mind you, this was well before the most recent violent clashes. So you see, Mr Ionescu, perhaps you are not quite aware of what the Romanians really want...'

'Let me get this straight, General. Are you saying that if it's the will of the people, you and your organisation are ready to launch a military coup?'

'Mr Ionescu, all I am saying is that we are prepared to help whoever is in power to understand the true purpose of the army in our society.'

53

The Prime Minister was half an hour late for his appointment with the President. His senior adviser (and part-time lover) had warned him that they were planning to get rid of him and that he needed to get his act together. He had been PM for just over a year, but he still found it difficult to get used to all the political manoeuvring required. The President didn't seem at all perturbed by his tardiness, invited him to sit down and sat down himself on a stool in front of him.

'My dear man, I have to admit that I am facing one of the most difficult challenges of my political career. I have nothing with which to reproach you, you've been one of the best prime ministers this country has ever had. But for the good of the state, I have to dissolve this government. You see, the truth of the matter is that Varlaam's words and activities have started gaining more and more support from the army over the past ten days. Dulgheru's suicide caused incredible friction, and there is a real fear of military insubordination after the incidents at Victoria Palace. To all intents and purposes, we are facing a mutiny in the army ranks, provoked by the problems within the Ministry of the Interior, the resignation of the minister, the suspension of eight senior officers and the inquiry into Commander Movilă's handling of the Dulgheru case. We have reason to believe that there have been leaks at senior levels from both the army and the intelligence services to people in Varlaam's organisation. We've heard that emergency cells of the St George's Association are forming in several counties. Have you heard about them?'

'Not really, no.'

'It's a kind of information network created by retired General Dumbrava, who secretly dreams of Romania following the example of the Turkish army, regulating politics and society, and with him at the top of the pyramid. He's a madman, mostly harmless, but he is a good orator and could cause some trouble. To top it all, we've also had messages from France, Germany, USA, asking us to show moderation and maintain stability at all costs. And the only way we can do that is to call for a government of national unity. Of course, that means we have to invite Radu Rădulescu and his party to be part of the new government and there is no way he would accept to be part of it if he weren't the prime minister. So here is what I propose for you. You can either choose to become deputy prime minister, overseeing economic development, or else you could become my presidential adviser, responsible for the economy. I don't want to create the impression that we are punishing you in any way. I've spoken to Rădulescu and he has agreed to thank you personally for all your hard work as prime minister.'

A moment of silence. 'Tell me, Mr President, when did you decide all this?'

'Almost immediately after Varlaam's attack.'

'That was two days ago. Don't you think that you are telling me all this a little late, too late to ask for my co-operation in this matter?'

'Prime Minister...'

'Let me be clear, Mr President. I already knew what you were planning. When I heard about it, I couldn't believe it. Not that you are replacing me with Rădulescu – I don't care about that. But that you didn't call me in to discuss it before discussing it with Rădulescu. That you didn't ask for my opinion and agreement to this political move. I might be quieter, less aggressive than some others in your party, but I am not a decorative object that you can move around whenever and wherever you please. I'm not a pawn on your chess table. You know full well what I gave up in order to lead the government when you asked me to do so. I was on track for appointment to a very senior position in an international organisation and was extremely well paid. But you convinced me that it was my moral duty to think of my country rather than of myself. That I needed to help you to get Romania out of its quandary. Well, don't you think it would have been your moral duty to ask for my approval to play this political game now? You might not have felt compelled to by the law, or by the need to maintain personal relationships, or the fact that I was – you said it yourself – the best prime minister you ever had. But don't you feel any moral obligation at all? Don't worry, Mr President, I won't cause you any problems. I'm not going to barricade myself in Victoria Palace and issue threatening statements. But I will never again collaborate with you.'

'I can see you're angry but…'

'It's not anger. It's profound sadness. Because you've proven to me yet again that it's not good enough to be qualified, professional, well-intentioned and to work your socks off … it still won't get you the respect you deserve.'

'I can understand you're feeling angry, but it was patriotism which made you accept this position last year, and you should let patriotism be your guide now. I may have let you down as a friend and as a human being, but I was entirely justified to do so as the President of Romania. Rădulescu is starting to destroy Varlaam's party. He got his people to provoke a rebellion in six counties. Plus, Rădulescu has a good relationship with the more conservative elements within the army, so that will help calm down matters. It could be an own goal for me personally, because having Rădulescu in government could give him brownie points and help him in the next elections. But we are too far gone now. I need to act like a responsible statesman to avoid danger. I am very sorry that you are turning down my two alternative offers. I wasn't trying to buy you off, I sincerely meant that I could do with your help. Anyway… Thank you for being a perfect gentleman and for refraining from making any public statements about this decision. What else can I say? Merry Christmas! Oh, and by the way, you said you already knew about this decision. Might I ask where from?'

'From someone very close to you,' the Prime Minister answered, pleased that he'd managed to get this small act of revenge, making the President anxious about who might be betraying him.

54

The inaugural meeting of the newly-appointed Cabinet lasted less than two hours. Radu Rădulescu was giving a press conference in front of the jostling crowds of journalists. He was accompanied by the new government spokesman.

'Thank you all for attending this session in such numbers, given that it is New Year's Eve. But of course, the news never sleeps, as they say. I would like to praise the maturity of Romania's political class, who all came together at this difficult time. Creating a government of national unity, with the leader of the main opposition party at its head, is indeed proof that we have surmounted our personal vendettas and moved beyond our petty political quarrels. I am pleased to see that we have all come to the conclusion that our disputes and sharp retorts in parliament are not helping to move this country forward and to solve our citizens' problems. By coming together in a political consensus, we have dealt a massive blow to extremism, xenophobia and political violence. I would like to thank the former Prime Minister, for his wisdom and courage in leading this country over the past year. I would also like to thank the previous

Cabinet for their work, but above all I would like to thank the members of this newly formed Cabinet for their courage. Our main task at present is to act firmly against any attempt to destabilise the country, and to stand strong against any intolerance and extremism. Before I answer your questions, please allow me to wish every single Romanian citizen a happy new year, a peaceful and joyous one. I would also like to wish all of you journalists gathered here today a very good year as well. And now, your questions, please. But please keep them brief, we all have New Year's celebrations to attend, no doubt!'

'Prime Minister, how will this collaboration with the current President influence you in the upcoming elections? After all, you'll be campaigning against each other then?'

'Believe me, both the President and I are fully aware of the possible impact this could have on the next elections. But this is not about electioneering and about which one of us is going to win. We need to be responsible politicians and find a feasible solution to the current crisis in Romania. Who knows, maybe after the elections, I will be President and the President will be Prime Minister...'

'What are you going to do about Theodor Varlaam?'

'We have to handle this with great care. In our hurry to do good, to correct things which are deemed illegal, we have to be careful not to commit illegalities ourselves. There has been a lot of speculation in the press, but we have to dig deep to uncover the truth of the matter. There are several ongoing investigations ordered by the government and, separately, by the parliament. Once we have the full results, we can take action.'

'Are the rumours true, that you are going to name Commander Movilă your personal adviser for internal affairs and policing?'

'Commander Movilă is a very competent man. I haven't quite decided yet, but there is a possibility he might become my adviser. '

'But wasn't he implicated in the attempt to cover up Dulgheru's involvement in the shooting?'

'Let's not jump to conclusions and sentence someone before their guilt has been proven, shall we? I suggest we postpone this discussion until we have more clarity in this matter.'

'A couple of months ago, you accused the government of inefficiency and incompetence regarding the Sword case. More than that, your close ally Nenișor Vasile hinted that there might be a conspiracy involving the former Minister of the Interior. How are you going to handle the case now that you are Prime Minister?'

'I discussed this very matter with the new minister last night. He's a very capable man, I have complete faith in his abilities. He promised me that I would have a full report about this case as soon as possible. He also promised that he would do his best to bring the matter to a speedy conclusion. We absolutely need peace and stability right now.'

'Now that you are Prime Minister, will you be investigating the way the executive has acted over the past three years, while you were in opposition? You kept accusing them of not respecting the law.'

'My main mission as PM is to ensure that the executive operates effectively. I will also be responsible for the global issues facing Romania and my focus will be primarily on extinguishing any manifestations of extremism and ensuring stability. Of course, if I come across any illegal activities that have been committed by the government in the recent past, I will take the necessary measures.'

'How do you get on with the President?'

'What do you mean?'

'Well, you've been political opponents, even enemies, for such a long time. You're always attacking each other. How do you think you will get on, now that you have to work together?'

'We will work together like two mature politicians who know that the only reason to go into the business of politics is for the collective good. I won't tell you that I've suddenly become best buddies with the President. But what I can tell you is that over the past few days, we've discovered that the things that unite us are far more important than the things which divide us.'

'So how will you campaign against each other in ten months' time?'

'Like true gentlemen. That's all for now. Thank you and see you back on the third of January.'

55

It was the last day of the year but Cotroceni Palace was still in turmoil. The President was supposed to record a New Year's Message to the Nation, and he didn't like any of the three speeches proposed by his advisers. He was in a grumpy mood. He didn't like power sharing with Rădulescu, he didn't like the criticism levelled at him by his political allies, who resented being removed from certain key positions to make way for a government of national unity. He didn't like being forced to compromise.

The film crew were waiting patiently in the main office. They'd prepared the backdrop: the Romanian and EU flags to the right, a tall Christmas tree to the left, soberly decorated. But the President was nowhere to be seen. He was hiding in the back office and editing his speech.

Speechwriter Marinescu was running between the front and back office, somewhat irritated but also rather amused, holding several pages of edited scripts. The President motioned to his security adviser to come closer.

'Have you told Marinescu yet?'

'Not yet. But I'm sure he'll accept. Argentina is a good embassy, he speaks Spanish, he'll like it. I'll tell him in the New Year.'

'And what if he turns it down?'

'Why on earth would he? We're not sending him to Africa, after all! I've got Australia as a Plan B, but I'm pretty sure he'll accept Argentina.'

'I thought he was keen to go to the States.'

'So are hundreds of others. I'm not going to appoint him ambassador there!'

'Not ambassador, but maybe a consul? We're planning to open several consulates in the States, so I think one of those cushy jobs would appeal to him.'

'O-kay... But let's try Argentina first. If he refuses, we'll think of something else. By the way, have you heard that Rădulescu is appointing ex-Commander Movilă as his special adviser? I consider that a direct attack on you. We're about to sanction the man, and he takes him on as a counsellor?'

'My dear friend, that's what it's going to be like for the next ten months. You don't really think that Rădulescu has had a sudden change of heart, do you? He's still the same brute he's always been. He doesn't love us and we don't love him. He'll try to screw us, we'll try to screw him.'

'Mr President, I'm sure I'm not the only one to tell you that I think you made a grave mistake.'

The President put down his teacup, stood up and went through to the kitchen. One of his members of staff walked up to him at once and asked if he could help. He didn't actually need anything, but he was looking for an excuse to end the discussion with his adviser. He didn't want to have to explain himself, he was fed up with politics and with the New Year's Message. He asked for a glass of juice and something to eat and returned to his back office. The security adviser took up the discussion precisely where they'd left it off.

'The threat of Varlaam wasn't quite as pronounced as you made it out to be, nor was a military coup imminent. General Dumbrava only has a few supporters and isn't capable of organising a piss-up in a brewery. There was no need to insist upon creating a government of national unity.'

'Oh, there was a need, my dear friend, more than you might imagine. There's someone else who can tell exactly what that need was, and that's Stoicescu from the Intelligence Services. Want to know why? Not because of Varlaam, or the military, or even the disapproval from abroad. No, it's simply that in the New Year, when the new parliamentary session starts, Rădulescu was going to introduce a motion of no-confidence because of the problems of the ethnic minorities in this country. And I'll let you into a little secret. That motion would have passed. Because the Hungarians are furious, and some of our coalition partners had already shaken hands with Rădulescu on this matter. Don't ask me how I know, but I know it. You can imagine who feeds me the information. So Varlaam's attack on the government came at precisely the right time. We were lucky, because there was no way that we'd have gone so far as to organise a fake attack ourselves. But, given the situation, I could go to Rădulescu and say how our country is in grave danger.

'Of course, Rădulescu himself knows that the danger isn't really all that serious, that it was just an unfortunate over-reaction to Dulgheru's suicide. But how could he turn down the olive branch I was holding out to him? How could he not take part in the initiative to unite with the president to combat extremism? Public opinion would have never forgiven him, both inside and outside the country. I had to choose between two evils. Either see my government fall because I was unable to control the ethnic situation in Romania. Or else give up part of my power to one of my most vocal opponents for the sake of national stability, thereby proving that I am putting the country's interests above my own.

'Believe me, I dread those weekly meetings that I'll have to endure with that man, but there was no other solution. Our allies had abandoned us and we'd have lost everything within a month. Now, however, if there are any further issues regarding Sword, it's Rădulescu's problem rather than mine. If Varlaam shouts about bad governance, it's once again Rădulescu's problem. The West doesn't like how he does certain things, too bad, my friend! Not my problem!'

'And if he manages to solve those problems?'

'Well, you can't avoid all risks.'

'What are we going to do about Varlaam?'

'Nothing.'

'What? Aren't we putting him in prison?'

'Good heavens, no! If we arrest him, then all his party members will migrate towards Rădulescu and strengthen his arm. But if Rădulescu is the one to decide to arrest him, then he will lose those voters. Anyway, Varlaam is no longer a problem. He's so afraid of being thrown into prison, that he'd be ready for a pub crawl with the Hungarians, if we asked him to. He keeps sending me messages about meeting up "for a chat". Same messages that he sends to Rădulescu. Let him stew in his own juice! He will only become relevant again in autumn, when he gets a certain number of votes. Those are not votes that he steals from me, by the way, far more likely to be from Rădulescu's voters. For us personally, it pays to keep Varlaam present but ineffectual. And if he does disappear, it shouldn't be done by us.'

Marinescu came in with yet another edited version of the script. The President didn't like it any better than the previous three, but he finally accepted it. They were ready to put it on the teleprompter and he could begin.

56

'Good evening, dear friends, and a Happy New Year to you all! May this coming year be better and more peaceful than the last one. And may God grant us a little bit of sunshine for a change! Our special edition tonight is all about the unexpected political changes that took place at the end of the year just gone. There's been a lot of speculation in the press about it, now that we are all back from the New Year's recess. Two op-eds caught my attention, and I'll quote from them at length.

'The first one is written by Ion Cârstea and entitled "Rădulescu's Mistake". I quote: *Freshly installed in Victoria Palace, Rădulescu now seems at pains to remind us just why he lost his presidential mandate three years ago in a humiliating defeat. He's ambitious and well-educated, but he has a fundamental flaw – he is easily influenced. He will always be persuaded by the last person he's seen. For the people around him, it's all about keeping your nerve and playing the long game rather than doing or saying anything strategic or significant. It must have been one of his special advisers who convinced him to name Movilă as a special consultant. Just to remind you: former Commander Movilă was Head of the Bucharest Police. He not only failed to catch the assassin known as Sword, but also falsified documents about the actions of Captain Dulgheru. Yet, believe it or not, he's appointed as a special adviser for internal affairs by the new PM, even though the former government launched a criminal inquiry into his activities. This is nothing less than personal defiance in the face of the President, and a blow to any notion of collaboration, upon which this entire concept of a government of national unity rests. To be honest, I am not terribly concerned about the President being attacked personally, because I think he deserves it. But I am concerned that these two political leaders are wasting their time on petty point-scoring instead of helping to get this country out of its current crisis. I was expecting Rădulescu to demonstrate how he is different to the current President. To be cool, collected, pragmatic and ready to co-operate to fulfil his mission. If he starts playing all these political games, then it was wrong of him to accept the prime ministerial position, and a bad move for the entire country.*

'So that's the first article that I wanted to refer to. I now move on to another op-ed written by Adrian Maier, entitled *I Fear Greeks Bearing Gifts*. Again, I quote: *I have no reason to believe in the patriotism of Romanian politicians, and especially not in the patriotism of our current President. I don't believe he cares about the common good, nor that his global vision goes beyond personal or party interests. I am convinced that his move at the end of last year, to create a government of national unity with the exclusion of the National Unity Movement, is born of keen calculations. Rădulescu's star was rising in the opinion polls, although he wasn't doing anything to deserve it. Basically, it's hard to make any mistakes when you are in opposition, and his popularity was soaring compared to that of the President. What to do? Well, simple: Rădulescu is no longer in opposition – he is now in power, put there by a president who can portray himself as a man full of integrity and non-partisanship, setting aside his personal feelings for the good of the nation. If things go wrong, it will be Rădulescu's fault, for not being as morally superior as the President. If it all goes right, it's thanks to the President's high moral principles. Furthermore, in the public perception, the PM's role is inferior to that of the President. So Rădulescu has willingly placed himself below the President, which may cost him in the future. I cannot help but repeat what our Latin ancestors said: Heaven protect me from those who come bearing gifts!*

'I have invited the two journalists who wrote these editorials here tonight. Thank you for coming, gentlemen! So, Mr Cârstea, according to your colleague here, this might all be part of the President's plan to discredit Rădulescu and lead to his defeat in the next elections...'

'Good evening and Happy New Year! Before we get into the subject matter, I would like to correct my esteemed colleague. It wasn't our Latin ancestors who used the expression about fearing Greeks when they bear gifts – they managed to beat the Greeks without any trouble. Rather, it was the Trojans who feared them, and we all know why. But never mind that. Adrian Maier launches an interesting hypothesis and I rather agree with it, which is why I said that Rădulescu is making some basic errors of judgement. When he was in opposition, the only errors that were visible were the presidential ones. As soon as the President made a mistake, Rădulescu's popularity would grow. But now, all eyes are on him. The part that I disagree with in Maier's theory is that the President did all this with premeditation. That would be far too strategic of him. I think he simply panicked when he heard of the attack on Victoria Palace and the verbal insults thrown at him by Varlaam. He came up with the only possible solution he could see – a government of national unity which would exclude the National Unity Movement. Nicely put, by the way! And Rădulescu saw this as an opportunity to raise his profile and be in prime position for the November elections, so he demanded the PM's job.'

'Mr Cârstea, thank you so much for your history lesson. When you have a busy schedule like myself, having to produce a daily paper with a circulation of four hundred thousand, then you don't have time for ancient history. I prefer to focus on recent and contemporary history. Which is why I have clear information that it was the President who proposed that Rădulescu become PM, and that the Victoria Palace attack was not a mere accident.'

'What are you insinuating?'

'Everything that happened there was just the way it was meant to be. The police left the scene at just the right time, the rioters went in at just the right time, they were removed from the building just in time, and as you know the twelve instigators identified by the crowds haven't been caught yet. Meanwhile, Varlaam is scapegoated for this set-up.'

'Set-up, by whom? I don't follow...'

'Set-up arranged by the President, who needed an excuse to place Rădulescu in a position where he starts losing points in the opinion polls.'

'Mr Maier, as a journalist myself and your TV host, I can assure you that the current President is incapable of quite such Machiavellian manipulation. I think you're mistaken.'

'Gentlemen, let's analyse this step by step, shall we? Why is it that the police disappeared for just long enough that the rioters were able to penetrate the building, and then they showed up just in time to expel them from the building after they set fire to a couple of things? Did you see how long it took them to clear the square when they finally decided to intervene properly? Less than five minutes! Why didn't they do that earlier? Next, why did the President invite Rădulescu to his emergency meeting just afterwards? It was right after that meeting that he proposed Rădulescu for the prime ministerial post. Surely, in a moment of national crisis, you don't invite your greatest enemy to sit down with you. You first need to analyse things, evaluate matters, reflect upon the consequences. But no – in less than forty minutes, the square was empty, the fires were extinguished and we were well on our way to having a new Cabinet with a new PM who just a few moments ago had been the leader of the opposition. This all happened in less than an hour!'

'So you are maintaining that the whole attack upon the government building was merely a set-up organised by the President and that Rădulescu fell into a trap? Are you going to say that the President convinced Varlaam to go to the square?'

'Of course not! I'm not going to say absurd things. Varlaam went there of his own free will, naturally. But I wouldn't put it past the President to infiltrate the ranks of the demonstrators with some troublemakers who suggested the attack on the building and the arson.'

'I have to say, Mr Maier, in my twenty plus years of journalism, I can be sure of one thing. Any conspiracy in Romania becomes public knowledge in less than twenty-four hours. If three people get together and have a secret, it will become publicly property in twelve hours. Besides, no Romanian is prepared to risk their position, fortune or freedom for an idea or for another person. It's my turn, therefore, to ask you to think about this carefully. You believe the President infiltrated the ranks of the demonstrators. How many people in total? Twenty or so? So that's twenty people he had to let into the secret. Then he had to tell the police forces about this plan, to get them to retreat. So that's another hundred or so people, and of course their superiors. He would also have to ensure that some special security forces were around to ensure that all is going according to plan and that they are not arresting the wrong people. Above all, he had to be sure that Rădulescu was going to accept his proposal. What would happen if after all that effort in putting on a show, Rădulescu had turned him down and asked for snap elections instead?'

'It would have harmed Rădulescu's reputation – that he didn't want to collaborate in the fight against extremism.'

'Fine, but it would have been an extremely risky strategy on the part of the President. Do you seriously believe that a few hundred people could have been involved in this conspiracy and yet no one has heard anything about that?'

'Of course we've heard about that – this is exactly what Varlaam was saying after the event.'

'Mr Maier, Varlaam said he had heard rumours that the President's security adviser had met one of the instigators in a pub. But who was this instigator? Do we have a name? Do we know what he looks like? How come he has been identified as an instigator, but no-one has caught him? Besides, the said security adviser was out of the country at the time this is supposed to have happened. Varlaam is not a credible source. He's merely trying to save his own skin, because he was the one who organised the protests, it was his crowd of rioters who attacked the building. The reason the police forces were reluctant to use force against the public in the first instance is because they were fully aware of the accusations that might be levied at them about excessive use of force after the whole Dulgheru case. Once the protestors entered the building, a superior officer instantly authorised the use of force, and they were able to push back against the demonstrators. All the President did was try to find a compromise solution, and Rădulescu accepted it because he hoped it would raise his profile. And he will be entirely successful, as long as he doesn't make stupid mistakes such as appointing controversial people such as Movilă.'

The show host interrupted the discussion. 'Excuse me, gentlemen, we have the President's security adviser on the phone right this instant.'

'Good evening. I have a very simple reason for calling tonight. I simply want to reassure viewers that, contrary to what they might want to believe, we at Cotroceni are not constantly engaging in complex conspiracies. I know that in American movies it's a recurring theme to show presidents and their teams engaging in sophisticated conspiracies, but that's not how we operate. I may not be able to convince Mr Maier, since he has clearly chosen to believe the unfounded accusations made by Varlaam. But I would like to convince your viewers that what happened at Victoria Palace was a planned attack by Varlaam's followers, and that the police forces hesitated to retaliate. I would also like to point out that similar attacks and demonstrations were being organised by Varlaam's party in other parts of the country, it was by no means a solitary incident. That's why the President decided that the best option would be to form a government of national unity without the participation of the party that was launching all these attacks, the NUM. This government has been operational for several days.

'You also mentioned my ostensible involvement in this conspiracy, so I would like to declare that I never had a meeting with any instigator of violence, and that anyone who states that I have done that should come with concrete evidence instead of rumours. Last but not least, I would like to say that I found this entire talk show incredibly offensive. Mr Cârstea's speculations cannot be proven false, and he has the freedom of speech etc. etc. However, you, Mr Maier, the statements you made are endangering our national security. If you should decide to tackle this subject again in the future, you should make sure you have real evidence instead of just accusations. Otherwise we might have to seek legal recourse. Thank you.'

57

The freshly appointed Minister of the Interior Ion Leşan heard about a new Sword victim just as he was about to enter the reception room at the ministry to celebrate his name day together with some of his colleagues. As he approached the closed doors, he could hear a band getting ready to play the traditional song for anniversaries and name days. Instead of entering the reception room laid out with food and drink, he was whisked off to the party headquarters where Rădulescu was waiting for him. On the way there, he was given some further details. The victim was Ion Donici, a loan shark enforcer, who had just got out of prison thanks to the general amnesty for petty criminals at the end of the previous year. He had probably been murdered a few days ago, but nobody had entered the property until today, the seventh of January, because it was St Ion. He had a long list of criminal offences, he was a gypsy and the MO was Sword's in every detail. There was no doubt about it. The mass media were already all over the story. There were no further clues, of course.

Rădulescu invited the new minister into his office at once. Nenişor Vasile and former Commander Movilă were there with him. Leşan was about to tell him all that he had heard about the case so far, but Rădulescu seemed to be well informed. Movilă added a couple of useless details, and then an uncomfortable silence fell in the room. The minister had chosen to sit in the armchair furthest away from the PM, while Nenişor was standing at the window, ostensibly watching the sparse snowflakes blown about by the wind. Movilă started smoking a cigarette, keeping his head down, sitting in his uncomfortable high-backed chair next to the PM's desk.

After a couple of minutes of silence, Rădulescu grabbed the heavy ash tray from his desk and lobbed it at the wall. The ashtray broke in half and a fairly large chunk of plaster fell onto the carpet.

'Imbeciles, good for nothings! What do you think? That I've come into power to allow you all to make fun of me? Is that why I gave you all these jobs and titles? For me to lose my percentage in the polls? For that illiterate jerk in Cotroceni to make fun of me? Do you think I'll put up with this nonsense? That guy comes along and kills whom he pleases and nobody stops him? Don't forget – if I fall, you all fall with me! Why are you here? Minister, why aren't you in an emergency meeting at your ministry and working hard on catching the criminal? Surely you don't think I'll keep you in position if you fail to do that! I'll kick you out and wipe the floor with your incompetence. You'll be so compromised that you won't dare to show your face again in public. This is no longer December of last year. Everything's changed now. I want you to go on national TV and make a solemn promise that you will catch Sword in ten days, or else you'll resign. I then want you to go to my secretary and have your resignation letter typed up and signed. Dated the seventeenth of January. If you don't arrest Sword by then, I will be overjoyed to accept your resignation. Dismissed!'

'Movilă, same thing, minus the TV appearance. When I named you special adviser, you promised to help me any way you could, given you were in a bit of a tight place. This is your first test of loyalty. Deadline: seventeenth of January. If the killer is not caught by then, you're out on your ear too. You don't need to write a resignation letter, because I'll just kick you out. In the meantime, kiss Cârstea's arse, so that he stops picking on you in his paper.'

The two men left the office in a hurry. One of the bodyguards came in to scoop up the broken ashtray and plaster and left without a word, head kept firmly down.

Rădulescu turned to his friend Nenișor.

'What the hell are we going to do? I thought it had stopped. There'd been no new murders in nearly two months.'

'Do you think those two are capable of catching the criminal simply because you yelled at them?'

'Of course not. But if they fail to catch him, I've got them lined up as scapegoats. It would be great if they did manage to catch him. Just imagine! If I manage to oversee the successful arrest of the man so many others have failed to catch, it's game over for everyone else. I will have succeeded where everyone else failed.'

'Who the hell is this guy? He clearly is very smart, but who could he be?'

'Nobody knows. Could be anyone.'

Nenişor sat down on the chair recently vacated by Movilă. An idea was beginning to form in his head.

'Listen, Radu. If it could be anyone, then it doesn't matter whom we catch, as long as we convince everyone that he's the criminal.'

'What do you mean? Find someone and claim that he is Sword? Won't he defend himself, deny it? That will make us look even worse than now.'

'If he gets a chance to talk... Don't forget, this is the most dangerous criminal Romania has ever known. He won't allow himself to be caught without a fight. And there's a lot that can go wrong during a fight.'

'You mean...? Hmmm... But there's a problem. The general public tend to sympathise with Sword, because he is cleaning up the country of gypsy criminals. If I'm the one to kill him, that will be a blow to my popularity. Especially after everything that Cornel Ardeleanu said about my birth mother.'

Nenişor looked his friend straight in the eyes and began to laugh. He'd found a solution. The perfect solution.

58

'Have you missed him? His legendary take-downs, his barbed wit – the only man in Romania who can make politicians tremble? Well, fear not, he's back! Even better, he's with us tonight – please welcome Alin Dobrescu!'

The hired extras in the audience burst into tempestuous applause while the band played a highly stylised version of the triumphal march from Aida. Dobrescu came down the stairs slowly. He didn't look relaxed or smiley, in fact he didn't look at all like a man hosting an entertainment show a week and a half after New Year's Day.

'Good evening, lovely to be back. Happy New Year to all of you and all those who were celebrating their name day during this period. If we take into account all of the important saint's days from the sixth of December through to the seventh of January, it feels like half of the population of Romania is celebrating continuously. We start drinking on the sixth of December and don't stop until pretty much today, January the tenth.

'But today we are finally sober. Our discussion tonight will therefore be a serious one, because it's on a topic that is far too important to make fun of it. An important topic for all of us, and for me personally. You might remember that a month or so ago I hosted a show about the major clean-up of criminal activities organised by the police. My guest was the Minister of the Interior at the time. I thought it was a good show, and the minister was very candid and said things politicians usually avoid saying. Of course, the very next day I was attacked by one of the major newspapers… No, no need to boo! The chap who attacked me is one of our best journalists writing today. Which is why I am ready to reply to him tonight. I am attacked daily and I don't bother responding to people who can't write, who put a comma between subject and predicate in a sentence. But Marius Ionescu is quite different. He is a talented journalist and I care about his opinions, which usually coincide with mine. After that show, Ionescu accused me of being an opportunist, that I probably had some financial gain from praising the minister. Well, that man is no longer a minister, so I don't have anything to gain any more, so this is the right time for me to respond to Ionescu.

'I honestly believe that the former Minister of the Interior was one of the best ministers that those thick-headed men in power ever had. I liked the fact that he stood up for his men, that he didn't make a fortune, nor did he promise impossible things. I even like the fact that he was working for the private sector company Cielo before becoming a minister and is now back to working for them. I agree with his gradual approach to harder sentences for criminals. No doubt you have your personal reasons for considering him a bad minister. But can you at least allow me to have my own reasons for considering him a good one? After so many years as a journalist, when you've seen me grilling so many politicians of all political persuasion, and after so many discussions over a beer in the pub, won't you give me credit for acting honestly?'

Dobrescu had finished his speech. Everyone was dumbfounded, the band, the audience, not even the studio producer knew how to react to this. There were a few isolated claps, a hesitant clash of the cymbals, but above all silence. Dobrescu smiled and relented a little.

'Well, taking all that into account, please allow me to present tonight's guest, Ion Leșan, the new Minister of the Interior, who's already facing his first major crisis.'

This time the others knew what to do. The band played, the audience clapped and the minister walked in, shook Dobrescu's hand and sat down in the armchair.

'I understand that Sword gave you a lovely little present on your name day. Just as you were about to sit down and enjoy your stuffed cabbage leaves, that man destroyed your appetite with a swoop of his sword. And it wasn't just the stuffed cabbage, there were patés and pickles, cold meats, grilled meats and even a massive cake.'

'I'm afraid I don't understand…'

'Neither do I. I was invited to your name day celebration – the one you never got to attend – and I have to admit I asked myself if it wasn't a little bit premature to have such a grandiose feast when you'd only just been appointed. All that was missing were the dancing girls! When I saw, however, that you abstained from attending and went instead into an emergency meeting with your police forces, I thought maybe there was hope for you yet. So tell me, minister, are you all about the feasting or is there something of more substance to you?'

'I'm from Transylvania, Mr Dobrescu. I'm not a big fan of grilled meat and feasting, I prefer simple fare.'

'A man of the people, then?'

'A prudent man. Call me stingy, even. Which might explain why I've cancelled the publicity contract you had with the Ministry of the Interior.'

'Why would you do that?'

'Because I don't have the money and because I'm stingy. As for that so-called feast – in Transylvania, it's tradition that the host pays for the nameday meal out of his own pocket. I bought all of that food myself, as a way to say welcome all my new colleagues. I'm glad you enjoyed it, because of course I didn't have a chance to do that.'

'Right. I see, you took away my contract, but hey, at least you fed me! Not bad for a stingy Transylvanian. So, how are you doing with Sword?'

'You're aware of my statement at the press conference: if the criminal isn't caught by the seventeenth, I will tender my resignation.'

'That's a bit short notice. My publicity contract might not be endangered after all... If you don't catch him, maybe your successor won't be a stingy Transylvanian.'

'Mr Dobrescu, allow me to make a suggestion. Put some trust in our police. They'll catch the bastard.'

'Do you have any concrete proof of that?'

'If I had, I wouldn't be spilling them out to you at this moment in time. Just wait until January the seventeenth and you will see. If I don't catch him, I leave. Simple as that.'

'They do say that Transylvanians are slow, stubborn, but that they keep their promises.'

'It's not about Transylvanians in general. There are certain types of people who keep their promises. There are plenty of Transylvanians who don't. But I do.'

'What's your honest opinion of your predecessor? Was he a good guy or a bad one?'

'I heard your monologue. And, as with every person, there's a lot of good and bad stuff that could be said about anyone.'

'Give us a taste of the bad stuff, then!'

'Let's just say that, from my point of view, the former minister's good points outweighed his bad ones. And I do appreciate the fact that he stood up for the police. He was fully aware of the impossible situation that police forces often find themselves in, and that only politicians and MPs can do anything about it.'

'Would you have resigned if you'd been in his place?'

'I'm ready to resign in my own place, thank you very much.'

'Yes, I heard your declaration earlier today. And I have to admit, it sounded a bit pathetic. Like a sermon at a funeral. Except the dead person, Sword's victim, was a criminal, let's not forget that.'

'You're wrong. The dead person was a victim pure and simple. Every victim deserves our attention. Sword is the real criminal and he needs to be caught.'

'Another question. Senior officers in the police are often accused of corruption and bribery. They have tiny salaries, yet seem to be able to afford fancy cars and huge houses. What are your plans? How do you stand, financially speaking?'

'I told you before. I'm a stingy Transylvanian, so I've managed to save up enough money. I already own a house and a Mercedes. I'll leave this position with as much money as I came in, and no more.'

'Indeed. Well, I'm pretty sure that no one would be able to make much of a fortune in the seven days you still have left in position.'

59

The presidential plane had landed on the tarmac a few minutes earlier and the President emerged looking reasonably cheerful, with ruffled hair. He always took a nap on the plane, and never quite managed to comb his hair well enough afterwards. He greeted his aides at the foot of the steps, exchanged a few amiable remarks with the ministers who had accompanied him on his trip and then stepped into the VIP lounge, where he gave a short address to the gathered journalists. He answered some questions and ended on a high note with a joke, then he gave a short personal quote for national TV, another for a prominent newspaper. He got into a limousine together with his security adviser and left the airport.

'So, can it be really true? They managed to catch Sword?'

'We can't be entirely sure, but our sources in the police inform us that Rădulescu and Leşan left no stone unturned in their efforts to get a serious lead in the affair. Leşan said he would hand in his resignation if he failed to catch the criminal by the seventeenth – and it's the twelfth today. It appears that Movilă holds some of the cards, and that he's given them to Rădulescu in exchange for being made his special adviser.'

'We should have got rid of Movilă a while ago...'

'I told you so. Movilă and the former minister. Anyway, the new Minister of the Interior is a good guy. I saw him on Dobrescu's show two days ago – he's a good speaker, seems open and assertive, very persuasive. And if they really do catch Sword... well, it's game over for us.'

'What information does Stoicescu have?'

'He confirmed there is some buzz coming out of the police, but he wasn't able to establish anything concrete. The police never co-operated much with the intelligence services, and now that Rădulescu is in power, they are even less co-operative. All he can tell us is that they appear to have stumbled upon something.'

'What is the likely impact? What can I do?'

'There's just one good thing in all this. Namely, the whole issue about Rădulescu's birth mother. If they catch the guy, and he really is what we believe him to be, and he starts saying what we believe he will say, then public opinion will not be kind to Rădulescu.'

'Yes, but I can hardly be seen to be supporting the killer...'

'No. But all you have to do is not say a word. Since you put Rădulescu in charge as PM, the front pages are no longer full of you – it's no longer about your successes or your shortcomings. It's all about Rădulescu.'

'Not quite true. I see that your friend Maier and Cârstea and Ionescu are starting to fall back into their old habits of cursing me. And if Rădulescu manages to catch Sword, that is a huge positive point in his favour. He will demonstrate just how efficient he is. Meanwhile, we are being hung out to dry with our collaborators and their demands.'

'Speaking of which, Marinescu is not keen on Argentina.'

'Why on earth?'

'He says it's too far away. But I have found a compromise solution which he has accepted in principle, but you need to pull a few strings.'

'Don't tell me we're opening a consulate in the US especially for him?'

'No, but you have to bring home an ambassador. Not a biggie, he's been in the position for rather a long time anyway.'

'OK. I'll have a think about it. Anyway, be prepared. If they fail to catch him by the seventeenth, I want all of the press that's on our side to demolish them. The minister and Rădulescu above all. Front pages, editorials, radio news, TV reports, letters from viewers and all that jazz. I want them trampled into the dust!'

60

'Irina here to present breaking news. The search for the most wanted criminal in Romania in recent history is over. As we mentioned in previous special editions of the news, this morning police SWAT teams raided the home of the criminal known as Sword. After a brief exchange of gunfire, the criminal realised that there was no chance of escape and put a bullet through his head. The house raid was conducted with the utmost secrecy, so we don't have a lot of further details. All I can tell you is that the Ministry of the Interior has assured us that none of their people were injured during the operation and that Ionel Nicoară, the person who died in the raid, was undoubtedly the man known as Sword. The notorious murder weapon was found on the premises, and was taken to the forensic lab for further examination.

'We have done our own research, of course, into Ionel Nicoară. He was born in 1966 and has worked as a rubbish-collector. He was currently unemployed. He had been admitted three times to hospital with mental health problems. He had no criminal record. He was a Romanian citizen of Roma origin, he was not married and lived alone. Our reporter Dan Dumitrescu is at Nicoară's house. Dan, what are the neighbours saying? What is the word on the street about the Sword case now?'

'Good evening, ladies and gentlemen. Zimbrului Street was always a peaceful place, without any problems. I spoke to a retired gentleman who's been living here for over forty years. In all this time, the only excitement they've ever had was the earthquake in 1977, which destroyed the chimneys of two houses, and a fire in 1985. This morning, however, the neighbours woke up to gunfire and special assault troops smashing down doors. According to eyewitnesses, at around six o'clock this morning a number of cars stopped in front of number twenty-one, where Nicoară lived. Approximately ten armed men, dressed head to toe in black with balaclavas over their faces, got out of the cars. They smashed in the doors, you could hear furniture being overturned and then the sound of automatic weapons. After around ten minutes, the special units left and the ordinary police took their place, cordoning off the area around the house. Nobody has been able to go inside the house, other than the forensic team. You can see it is still off-limits.'

'How do the neighbours feel, knowing that such a notorious criminal was living in their midst?'

'To my surprise, some of the neighbours were not really aware of the Sword case. Others were very surprised to hear that Nicoară was the wanted man. They told me that he was a quiet man, who kept himself to himself, rarely got into any arguments, that he was polite and respectful. Very reserved.'

'Are there any further developments there?'

'No, the street seems very quiet and the only indication that something happened here earlier today is that there are still police guards posted outside number twenty-one.'

'Thank you, Dan. We are now on the phone with the Minister of the Interior, Mr Ion Leşan. Good evening, sir, and congratulations on capturing one of the most dangerous criminals Romania has ever known.'

'Thank you. Of course it's not me, but the police, the SWAT teams and the intelligence agencies who deserve to be congratulated.'

'A few days ago you said you would hand in your resignation if you failed to catch the killer. Did you already have some good leads at that time?'

'No. But I felt that we needed to focus all our collaborative strength, that we needed to show how seriously we took our jobs and send a clear message that we would do everything in our power to ensure the safety of our citizens. Romania has a relatively low crime rate compared to other European countries, and we'd like to keep it that way.'

'Are there any further details that have not been made public?'

'Not really. There may be some details missing from our official statement about the intelligence gathering operation, but the case has been investigated with full transparency.'

'Have you found the murder weapon?'

'Yes, the weapon is now in our hands. And I can confirm that it has been identified as the weapon used in all of the murders.'

'And is it true that Nicoară was in fact of Roma origin?'

'Yes, that's true.'

'Thank you, Minister, and once again, congratulations!'

'Thank you, Irina, and I'd also like to thank the Romanian press for their help in catching the criminal.'

'Well, ladies and gentlemen, the Sword case has kept us on tenterhooks since last summer when the first body was found. The killer had the same MO in every case and the victims all shared two characteristics: they were of Roma origin and they all had criminal records. The case soon became heavily politicised, with some accusing the police of siding with the killer. Towards the end of the year, there was an escalation of interethnic conflict and several people became the victims of intolerance and hate crimes. So, in addition to the eleven known victims killed directly by Sword, another seven people lost their lives in these violent clashes, while tens of others were injured and material goods worth several million lei were destroyed. This case showed just how fragile our democracy really is, and how easy it is to destabilise our politics. I've invited Mr Laurenţiu Petre from the Romanian Information Bureau into our studio, to discuss the psychological repercussions of this case. Good evening, Mr Petre, nice to have you back!'

'Thank you.'

'Six months ago, when you first appeared on TV, you launched the hypothesis that the killer could be of Roma origin. This was very badly received at the time. Six months later, it appears that you were right. How did you come to this conclusion back then?'

'I based it upon my research into serial killers worldwide. You see, in Romania we like to believe that we are truly unique. But in fact there are a lot of similarities with what happens elsewhere in the world. Both good things and bad things. It is counterproductive to discount other people's experiences, simply because we believe that we are special and different. Otherwise we risk reinventing the wheel every single time.'

'So, coming back to Sword, does the psychological profile of the killer seem coherent to you? A quiet, retiring man, never in any trouble with the law, no past problems, yet he kills eleven people in six months.'

'Who says no past problems? We heard that Nicoară was hospitalised three times with mental health issues. If we were to analyse his medical records, I'm sure we'd find signs that would indicate increasing violence.'

'I'd like to point out to our viewers that we are going to be talking to one of the doctors who treated Nicoară shortly afterwards.'

'And there's more. From what I've heard, he comes from a broken home. His father had been in prison several times, which would explain the contempt he felt for criminals. There are many serial killers in history who appeared to lead blameless lives, model citizens in their way. I told you before about Ted Bundy, who was part of his neighbourhood watch team. Just to mention one of the best-known recent serial killers.'

'So, as far as you can tell, Nicoară fits the profile of a serial killer?'

'My dear lady, a serial killer often hides beneath an apparently normal façade. A good neighbour, someone you would trust with your own child. That's the kind of person Nicoară appears to have been. And that's why he was so difficult to find. If he'd been the kind of violent person who is constantly causing trouble in his neighbourhood, the police and the public would have been aware of him long ago.'

'You were severely criticised when you initially said that it could well be that Sword is of Roma origin. Why do you think that happened?'

'Simple. That's because we have the tendency to over-politicise things. We like to believe in conspiracy theories, occult influences and the like. The Roma MP Nenişor Vasile thought he was doing his ethnic group a favour by refusing to accept any scientific evidence about the possible identity of the killer. And he was wrong to do so. I'm not blaming him, but the escalation of conflict between ethnic groups certainly led to the serious incidents in Constanţa, Movila and in front of the government building. If these hadn't happened, we might have been able to save several lives. What we need to learn from this case is that the future holds many challenges. We are just at the start of our democratic journey and there are many related secondary phenomena and consequences that we cannot even begin to anticipate. There will be far more complicated crimes heading our way. We have to handle them with maturity and professionalism, rather than fling accusations at each other.'

61

It had been a harsh winter. It snowed almost every day in January. Towards the end of the month, there had been a bit of a thaw, there'd even been temperatures above zero in the daytime, but then overnight the blizzards started again and lasted for more than a week. Certain parts of Bucharest were completely snowed in, and there were many roads that had become impassable because of ice and piled-up snow.

In February there were a few warm days, when spring was in the air, temperatures soared to fifteen degrees and the trees were suddenly in bloom. People were going to work in trench coats or suits rather than thick winter coats. But then in March the cold struck again. More snow, more blizzards, more ice. It seemed to take forever.

It was April now and much better outside. The earth was still damp after so much snow and ice melting, but the grass had turned green and so had the trees. The air seemed much cleaner, the sky beamed blue, there was a pleasant breeze blowing from the forest, and temperatures were just about right, neither too hot nor too cold.

SWORD

Sergeant Liviu was doing his round together with two soldiers. They'd been deep in conversation, talking about women. One of them, Parjol, had just found out that the woman he planned to marry had left him for his cousin. He wanted to rush back home and beat both of them up, but of course he didn't have leave. What could Liviu tell him? Parjol was just nineteen and she'd been his first girlfriend. He had improvised a metal ring for her, they'd made marriage plans… and now here she was with his cousin. She'd sent him the ring back and said that she didn't want to see him again. Stupid girl! She could have just not said anything, done her business and not got this young boy all het up. He was so naïve and inexperienced, and he took it all so seriously that it had even upset his stomach. Every ten minutes, he would ask them to stop and he would go into the forest for a dump. Then he would hurry back and start all over again. He'd tell them how he'd rush back home in secret, go to his cousin's place and catch them at it, then beat them up util they were black and blue. He had the key to his cousin's flat, because that's where he used to meet his girl.

Then he had to rush back into the forest, because his stomach was hurting so badly. He'd get over it. As long as he wasn't foolish enough to attempt to desert his unit, because that would get him into serious trouble and she wasn't worth that.

The other youngster, Micky, was a quiet lad. He had one weakness: football. That was all he could talk about. He was from Olt county and a big Craiova supporter, so he lived for match days. He'd catch them on telly if he could. If not, he had a pocket radio with earphones and would listen to the games. He knew all the players, all the transfer gossip, the history of the club, the line-ups, how they'd missed their opportunity against Benfica Lisbon and so on and so forth.

While they were waiting for Parjol, ?Micky started talking about tomorrow's game. The sergeant let him have his say, would just interject every now and then that Rapid was quite a good team, merely to hear the other one get all agitated and say that Craiova was a much, much better team.

'Where the hell is Parjol? He's so skinny, how much shit can be left in him? See what nerves can do to a man? Go and see what he's up to!'

But just then Parjol appeared at the edge of the forest and made a sign that they should come over to him. He hadn't even bothered to pull up his trousers properly. He's lost his mind, the sergeant thought to himself. When they reached him, they saw he was white as a sheet and trembling. He pointed to the ground a few metres away, beneath the trees, where a body lay, with a single gaping wound in its throat.